THE DARK LADY OF TINTAGEL

QUEENS OF THE MIST - BOOK ONE

K. A. MILTIMORE

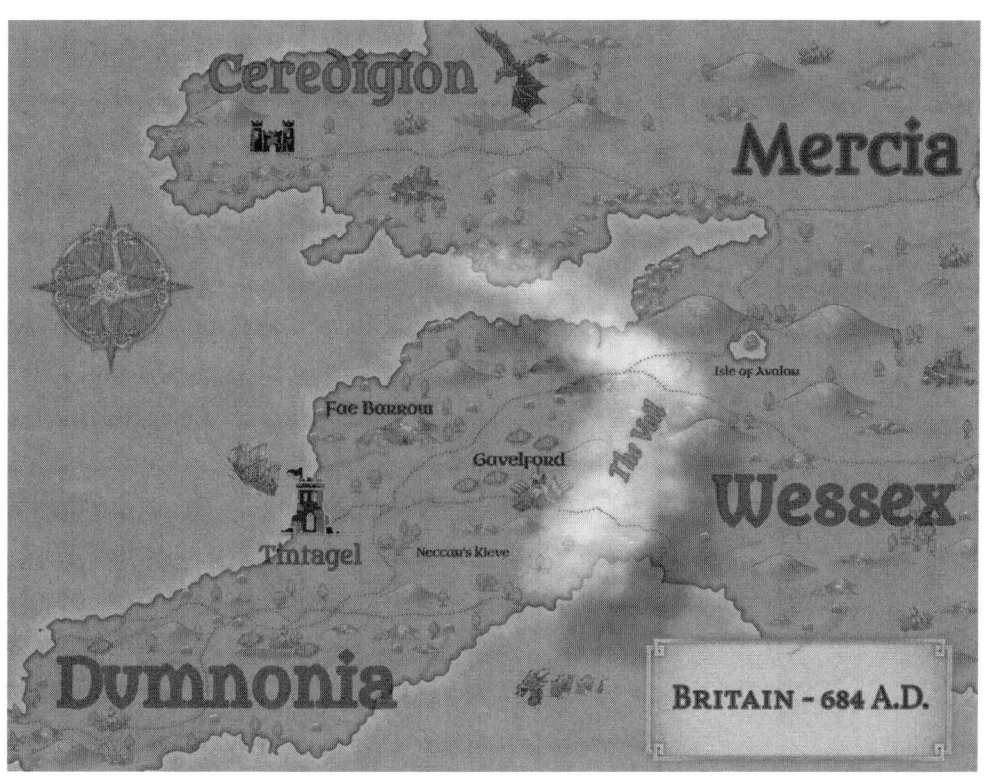

All rights reserved. This book or parts thereof may not be reproduced in any form, stored in any retrieval system, or transmitted in any form by any means—electronic, mechanical, photocopy, recording, or otherwise—without prior written permission of the publisher, except as provided by United States of America copyright law and for brief quotations for book reviews.. For permission requests, write to kamiltmore.author@gmail.com.

ISBN: 9798681010067

This book is a work of fiction. Any references to historical events, real people, or real places are used fictitiously. Other names, characters, places and events are products of the author's imagination, and any resemblances to actual events or places or persons, living or dead, is entirely coincidental.

CONTENTS

Chapter 1	1
Chapter 2	7
Chapter 3	13
Chapter 4	19
Chapter 5	23
Chapter 6	29
Chapter 7	35
Chapter 8	41
Chapter 9	49
Chapter 10	55
Chapter 11	61
Chapter 12	67
Chapter 13	73
Chapter 14	77
Chapter 15	83
Chapter 16	89
Chapter 17	93
Chapter 18	99
Chapter 19	109
Chapter 20	115
Chapter 21	121
Chapter 22	125
Chapter 23	131
Chapter 24	135
Chapter 25	141
Chapter 26	149
Chapter 27	157
Chapter 28	165
Chapter 29	171
Chapter 30	177
Chapter 31	183
Chapter 32	187

Chapter 33	197
Chapter 34	203
Author's Note on Historical References	205
Cast of Characters	207
About The Author K. A. Miltimore	209
Books By This Author	211

CHAPTER ONE

MAY 684 - CASTLE TINTAGEL, KINGDOM OF DUMNONIA

"Lady Igraine, your father is looking for you." Edith's voice rang out in the kitchen garden, where Igraine hid among the lavender and bee balm spring shoots. Her book lay unopened in her hand.

"I see you, Mistress, do not think your magic is good enough to render you invisible. Not yet, at least." Her chortles were almost as large as the woman herself.

"Yes, Edith, I am coming. I hate to leave the patch of sunlight just yet. You can't blame me for that, surely." The young woman's fingers traced the rocky earth, every pebble and stone a reminder that they sat perched on a cliff at the end of the world.

"He'll not appreciate you dawdling. Sun or no sun, Master Merlin waits with him." Her voice sounded reverent for the teacher and sorcerer, and Igraine squinted toward her across the garden patch.

"As I said, I am coming. You've done your duty, Edith. You've found the errant princess." Igraine clamped the dirt one last time and pushed off from her seat of dry stone and soft moss.

"They are in the turris. I would make haste Lady if I were you."

With a wipe of her apron to her brow, Edith left the sunlight for her kitchen's gloom and the heat from the cooking fire.

Igraine bent and took a quick pluck of a tiny mint shoot and rubbed it between her fingers. The scent of mint always calmed her. It wouldn't be long before summer came; the solstice was only next month. Everything in Igraine's world would change then, like it or not. She dropped the shoot and ambled toward her beckoning father in his stronghold.

It might have been mid-May, but the Dumnonian coast never really seemed to release the castle from the ocean's cold winds. They buffeted the fortress's thick walls day and night, piercing the stone and shale that led to the small isthmus between the mainland and the headland where the turris perched. Igraine liked to imagine that Tintagel was some legendary giant, a creature straddling the large ravine, with one foot on the point and one on the rugged cliffside. All the workshops, houses, stables, and guard towers, built on one side of the divide, with farms and pastures on the other - and all for the service of King Geraint. After all, everyone was at his service - servant and princess alike.

Her shadow, Longshanks, had decided to join the walk, and he drew Igraine from her moody thoughts. *It is impossible to be brooding on a sunny May day with a loyal mouser at your side, she thought.* Besides, there were enough comings and goings that she would surely trip or barge into someone along the way if she didn't pay attention.

"Good day, My Lady," a voice called out, as Igraine walked near the basin where the woman was soaking laundry. "I see your page trails behind you, looking dashing as always. Good day, Longshanks."

"Indeed, he cuts quite a figure, I would agree. Good day to you as well. Has the galley arrived, do you know?"

"Yes, she arrived today, loaded to the rails, or so I have heard. Good thing too because we're running low on soap. Nothing works as well as the soap from Byzantium." The woman gave the cloth in the basin a poke with a stick for emphasis.

"Thank you for the news," Igraine called back to her as she picked up her pace. The return of *The Gloria* was a cause for celebration.

If she had been more aware of the bustle around her, she would have known the answer to her question right away. Men were carrying clay amphoras; those giant handled jars filled with wine or olive oil. Tintagel's residents only saw that when the galley was back from its run to Byzantium.

"Shouldn't you be studying your spells, Princess?" A voice called from the doorway, causing Igraine to jump and step on Longshanks. He bolted with a hiss, and she grabbed the wall to avoid tripping on the raging feline.

"By Danu's grace, you startled me," Igraine said, irritation quickly flaring on her face but then melting away. She hadn't seen him in months. He looked the same except for the burnt skin and extra freckles on his face. The same shock of red hair, same lopsided smile, same tall frame. Same Arthur Spear.

"My apologies, Lady. I did not expect a powerful sorceress to be startled by the likes of a ship's deckhand."

"I'll see to it you are flogged, sailor," she replied, sounding imperious. He had the good grace to attempt a sheepish look, but it failed as easily as Igraine's mock ire.

"My Lady is always right," he said, with a bow and a broad smile.

"I'll forgive the trespass if you have my gift." Firmly back on her feet now, Igraine felt the swish of Longshanks' tail against her ankle. He'd come back from his furor with a reminder that she was being summoned.

"A gift? Was I supposed to bring you a gift? Some kind of offering to the Lady of Tintagel?" He patted his tunic as if he were searching for pockets to explore. His hair had grown long on the voyage to Constantinople, and it brushed against his eyelids.

"Not only do you startle me, now you mock me. I must be mad to keep you as a friend." Igraine pivoted on her foot as if to leave, but Arthur's smile never wavered. She had teased him so since childhood. They had grown up together within Tintagel's walls - a lonely princess playing with the son of the cook.

"Alright, Lady, I will not tease you. Yes, of course, I have your gift. Don't I always?" Every voyage since joining the crew, he had brought her some trinket from their ports of call. They were always small prizes; nothing beyond a sailor's means, but Igraine had cherished them just the same. She had never left Tintagel's lands, but she longed to one day.

From a pocket in his trousers, he pulled out a small silk pouch. He placed it gently in Igraine's outstretched palm, cracking that lopsided smile more broadly than she had ever seen.

"A gift befitting a princess. You can thank Hereca for the selection when you see her. I was going to go with the mummified hand I found in Carthage."

Igraine drew open the pouch and saw the red immediately. The brooch slipped from the silk into her palm, and she gasped. It was in the shape of an eagle and made entirely of garnets and gold. *It would have cost a fortune, a fortune that Arthur did not have.*

"Arthur, it is beautiful, but however did you acquire it?" Igraine picked it up with her other hand and held it close to inspect the glittering gems in the fading light. It was the most precious jewelry she owned.

"As I said, you can thank Hereca for that. She didn't tell me how she acquired it, and I didn't ask. You know as well as I that you don't ask Hereca to explain herself."

Over Arthur's shoulder, Igraine saw one of her father's guards heading their way. The last thing she wanted was to get him in trouble for her tardiness. She would have to visit him later if she wanted to hear the tale of the voyage.

"Well, I am quite grateful. Please thank her for me. I have to hurry now, but I want to hear about the sailing. Can we meet later?" The guard was coming closer, and his eyes were fixed on Igraine.

"Thank her yourself when you come to *The Gloria* later. You know where she's docked." With a wave, he slipped away into the throng of people hurrying to finish their chores before they lost the daylight.

"Lady, your father waits." The guard said, walking the line between officious and surly. Igraine paused long enough to secure the brooch to her gown before she turned without a word toward the turris and her father's will.

As King Geraint's only child, Igraine had grown up sheltered and, if she were being honest, spoiled. She'd never had to cross her father, at least not about anything that mattered. She'd been allowed the run of the castle as a girl, playing with the children of servants, giving her tutors fits and dear Gisela a hard time. She might have been spoiled, but Igraine was never cruel, never unaware of the hardships that faced others who were not as lucky as she.

When Merlin came to court five years ago and offered a miracle to protect Dumnonia, Igraine had hardly paid attention; it was her father's purview, not hers. Merlin had come to Tintagel, warning them that unless a magic Veil was raised, Dumnonia would be destroyed by invaders. Igraine had only been a girl, and the politics of magic weren't as interesting as chasing butterflies with Longshanks. She might have cared more deeply if she had known her role to play in keeping Merlin's spell intact. The carefree princess now had a duty she alone could perform and from which she could not turn away. She missed those carefree days and thought of them often.

"Lady?" The guard spoke again as her pace slowed, lost in her head.

"I am coming. We mustn't keep the Lord of Tintagel waiting, I know." She shook the thoughts from her mind, pushing them deep into the corners to deal with later. "Lead on," she said.

CHAPTER TWO

The Lord of Tintagel was drinking wine and studying a map when Igraine entered the hall. Torches blazed near him, lighting the table to help his waning eyesight. Despite having a powerful sorcerer in his court, King Geraint was going blind.

Courtiers hovered near the edges of the room, clumped in twos and threes, murmuring amongst themselves. Near the table sat the sorcerer, with his apprentice at his right hand. None of them looked up as Igraine entered the room.

"And we are sure the line will hold? The Saxons have marched from Wessex into the village of Glastening, so my scouts report. They are at our door, hounds baying for blood." Igraine's father had a convex piece of glass in a gold handle that he held above the map to inspect what his eye could no longer see unaided.

"My Lord, the line will hold. Morgan and I have made the enchantments. The invaders will forget that Dumnonia and our coastline ever existed. The memory of this place fades away when one comes near the Veil we have crafted. It has held for five years now, just as I promised, and it will continue, as long as we tend to it regularly and adhere to the omens." Merlin's voice was low in tone as well as volume. *When you held the king's will in your hand, there was no need to shout, Igraine thought.*

"Ah, my errant daughter arrives. You would do better to heed your father's call, Igraine. We have been waiting for you." The king set down his spyglass and walked toward his high seat in the center of the room. Merlin and Morgan stayed where they were.

"My apologies, Father, I was delayed." Merlin's face was as inscrutable as ever, but Morgan gave her a small smile.

"No doubt the receipt of that lovely brooch caused the delay. Work of the Huns craftsmen, if I am not mistaken," Merlin said. He missed nothing.

"I don't have time to discuss jewelry. There are more important matters at hand. Uther Pendragon is coming in a fortnight. Your wedding is only weeks away, and we have much to do to prepare for it." His voice rose through the stone hall, and the courtiers stopped their chatter to listen.

"What is your command, Father?" Igraine knew very well the timetable of the next few weeks. She also knew there wasn't anything required of her beyond obedience.

"Your studies, you must be prepared for the ceremony. Have you finished them as Merlin instructed?" With a start, Igraine realized she had left the precious spell book back in the garden.

"I was attending to the book when I received your summons. I will be ready, Father." It was a tiny lie, but her father didn't need to know that.

"See that you are. This union must proceed with no problems, Igraine. The safety and future of the kingdom depend on it. The Veil protects us for now, but we must unite with Pendragon and fulfill the prophecy to ensure our security. Your duty as princess is clear, Daughter. Do you understand me?"

What was there to understand, Igraine thought. Her future had been decided by men - by her father, her teacher, by her husband-to-be. She had no say in the matter. She had known this for the last year, but it hadn't made the thought any easier.

"I understand, Father. Is there anything else you require, or may I resume my studies?" Igraine asked flatly.

"Yes, you may go." He waved his hand in a gesture of dismissal.

"And Morgan shall accompany you," Merlin said before Igraine could so much as turn on her heel. His apprentice moved from his side toward Igraine, smiling again softly.

"Let's retrieve your book, Lady," Morgan said as the pair left the hall to the men and stepped out into the coming twilight.

"Morgan, I don't require a nursemaid. I can find the book on my own." It had been several minutes of uncomfortable silence as they walked back toward the kitchen garden in the gathering gloom. Morgan took no offense at Igraine's snappish tone.

"I never thought that you did, Lady. To be truthful, this provides me with a means of escape. Cooped up in the hall with my father and the king for the whole afternoon has made me a bit crazed. I hope you don't mind if I accompany you." Her dark hair was braided into two long plaits that reached down her back. They stood out against the deep red of her gown.

"Morgan, I apologize for snapping at you. None of this is your fault. I know you are doing as you are told, the same as me." Morgan's legs were walking at twice the speed to keep up with Igraine's long gait, and she slowed slightly to let the short woman catch up. She might be the daughter of a powerful sorcerer, but she reminded Igraine of the heroine of her favorite bedtime story, tiny Joan of the Torch, Queen of the Pixies. *Maybe Morgan has pixie blood, Igraine thought.*

"Lady Igraine, I know you chafe at the studies placed on your shoulders. And I know my father can be...difficult to get along with when it comes to duty. But I hope you will think of me as a friend and less as someone to see to your education. I have few friends, and I would like to count you among them." Morgan paused, looking up at the young woman. She was younger than Morgan, but it wasn't her youth that

Morgan saw in her eyes. It was her naivete. The girl had been sheltered her whole life. She had no idea what hardship or sacrifice was like, but that was about to change, and it made Morgan sad to think of it.

"Morgan, if you are indeed my friend, I would ask you a question. You are a seer. Can you tell me if you too have seen the prophecy that Merlin claims will destroy us all if there is no magic Veil?" Igraine had never asked Morgan anything like this before. *Was the princess questioning Merlin's word, Morgan wondered.*

"Yes, I am a seer, but no, I was not given the vision that Merlin shared with your father. Merlin's skills surpass my own. When he told me of his vision and we journeyed to your kingdom, I never doubted what he saw. Do you doubt him now?"

"No, I have no cause to doubt him, but my life and the safety of this kingdom rest on the vision of a sorcerer. A vision we must take on faith. Merlin tells us that without me, our people will face destruction. It is a heavy burden to take on the word of a stranger."

"It's natural you should have questions and doubts. But what Merlin does, he does to protect everyone. I believe that and you should too."

Igraine said nothing, walking next to Morgan with her eyes fixed on the path ahead. Morgan didn't need to be a seer to know the young woman was troubled.

"Come, let's fetch the book before the light is gone, and then we can ask Edith for a bit of food before tonight's feast. I must admit, I am starving." Morgan tugged at the princess's sleeve, and they hurried back toward the garden.

"My Lady, which gown will you choose?" Gisela called to Igraine from the garderobe, where she was plucking options for the Lady of Tintagel to wear. Without looking up from her bedside, Igraine knew she would be holding a blue gown. Gisela always favored her in blue ever since she was a child.

"Whichever you decide, Gisela. It doesn't matter to me, truly. If my father wouldn't take offense, I would wear this," Igraine pulled at the skirt of her linen gown, still stained from the garden dirt and grass.

It was almost time to attend him in the Great Hall for the feast to celebrate the return of *The Gloria*, the kingdom's link to the outside world. *At least Arthur would be there, she thought, and the others that she'd come to know.*

"Fine, the blue it is. You always look well in blue. And it will look nice with that lovely brooch. A gift from your favorite sailor, no doubt." Igraine heard the smile in Gisela's words, and it forced one of her own. Everyone knew that Arthur was a particular favorite of the princess.

"No, Hereca didn't give me this brooch, although I hear she picked it out. I hope to get the story from her in the hall." Igraine stood up as Gisela came over, shaking her head in a mock scold. Igraine shrugged in feigned innocence.

"Say what you will, Lady, but I know you like the lad. And he is very likable, so why shouldn't you. Just be careful that your father doesn't see you two with your heads together, chatting away like old friends. I don't expect he will appreciate that." With swift hands, she drew the old dress off and had the new clothing on before Igraine could even respond. In the dim reflection of her copper mirror, Igraine could see the blue bright against her auburn hair. Gisela was right; blue was a good color for her.

"My father appreciates nothing I do, so why should this be any different. Enough chatter about him. Let's tie up my hair with some of those silk ribbons, and we'll be away to the hall." Igraine sat on the small stool near the copper mirror and pinned the brooch just above her heart. The garnets looked even more lovely in the torchlight. *How had Arthur managed such a prize, she wondered.* One way or another, she would get him to tell her, even if she had to ask Hereca to torture it out of him. Outside of her father and Merlin, Hereca was the only person within the castle who frightened Igraine.

"Lady, might I ask if there is news about your upcoming union? When shall we expect Lord Uther to arrive?" Gisela wove the ribbons into Igraine's hair with years of practice; she never pulled a hair in the process. She'd been plaiting Igraine's hair since Igraine was a young girl.

"Word is he will be here in a fortnight. He and his retinue will be here for the solstice."

"And then we will be away, to the land of Ceredigion and his fortress there? I hear they have dragons in those lands." Her fingers wove the strands tighter, drawing Igraine's hair back away from her face and shoulders. In only a few moments, her hair was bound tightly down her back, as was proper.

"I haven't been told when we will leave for his kingdom, but I suspect it will be soon after. And as for dragons, we can only hope. At least that will be something exciting to see." Igraine didn't want to think about Uther, or the union, or even a dragon sailing above the Ceredigion skies. She didn't want to think about anything; it would all be happening soon enough.

"As you say, Lady," was her soft reply, and Igraine turned to give her an embrace.

"Let's not fret about it. Tonight, we'll make merry and tease Arthur, perhaps drink a bit too much ale and dance a bit as well. There is nothing we can do about any of it, so let's not worry." With a kiss on her cheek, Igraine headed toward the door with Gisela following behind her. The older woman grabbed a small torch from a holder near the door, and the party of two headed into the night for the feast.

CHAPTER THREE

APRIL 1984 - THE CORNISH COAST OF GREAT BRITAIN - THE RUINS OF TINTAGEL

"You know you are only here for eight weeks or so, right? You must have packed enough to move here." The intake worker at the bus shelter sounded like he might be joking, but the young man wasn't sure. The older gentleman scribbled on his clipboard and made another count of the four duffle bags.

"I was a Boy Scout, so I'm always prepared," the young man quipped, hoping to crack a smile on the man's face. It didn't work.

"Aye, no surprise there. Americans always think they are coming to the rescue. Despite what you might have heard, we have shops here in Bossiney with items for sale. No need to pack your whole house to come to dig in the dirt." With one more quick scribble, he handed him a pink slip of paper and gestured toward a bus waiting on the roadside. *The bloke from America holding up the show with his luggage.*

"Thanks," the young man said, taking the paper and reaching for the straps to load up his gear. The worker waved him off.

"I've got it. Just get on the bus. We've got a schedule to keep to if you don't mind," he said, grabbing the straps in his massive hands. His accent was pure Cornwall - rolled Rs and quiet Hs - so different from the young man's west coast American voice. With a nod gesturing toward the bus, the worker took all of the bags and left the young man standing curbside.

"Now that Captain America has arrived, we can be off," the man said, following him onto the bus and plopping into the driver's seat. The rest of the riders were spaced among the first five rows, each taking their bench seat. The young man smiled and walked toward the next vacant spot, behind a woman with great black owlish glasses.

"We'll be at Tintagel village shortly, and you can rest up at the pub, have your dinner, and get acquainted. Tomorrow, I'll take you to the site to meet the crew. Normally, when I drive my tour bus, I'd give you the nickel tour and tell you of King Arthur and his conception here at Tintagel, but I suppose most of you know it already. For those who may have forgotten, King Arthur's mother, Igraine, lived in the castle until she was cruelly tricked into sleeping with Uther Pendragon, with the aid of Merlin, the magician. The deception led to the birth of Arthur. Tintagel has been famous ever since." He paused and took a quick nip from some kind of flask he had in a cubby under the wheel. With a lurch, the bus took off and headed southwest.

"Hello there," the owlish girl said, turning around to look at him. No one else on the bus had done so.

"Hello," he replied, shoving his hands into his pockets for warmth. The April air was chilly, and the driver hadn't turned on any heat on the bus.

"My name's Elsbeth, Elsbeth Winter. I am here from University College London. You're from America? I think everyone else on the dig this term is a Brit." The magnification on the glasses made her eyes the size of golf balls - dark green and white golf balls.

"Yes, I'm from America. The west coast, actually. Seattle." She nodded knowingly. "This is my first time in the UK. My name's Arty. Arty Drake." More nodding and blinking from Elsbeth.

"I hope you have time to tour around London a bit before you head back. So much to see, you'll hate yourself if you miss out before going home. I don't suppose we'll have much time for sightseeing around

Cornwall, though. I hear they work you hard on this project." Arty almost expected her to make some kind of hoot sound as she blinked and turned her head.

"Well, I suppose they cram in as much as they can while the weather is good. I'm happy to be here; I can sightsee after the semester." The bus jostled a bit, and Elsbeth swiveled her head to look out the window. It allowed Arty to pull his book out of his coat's inner pocket.

"Oh, that's a classic. And fitting, since we are at Tintagel. 'The Once and Future King by T.H. White.' Classic." Arty nodded with a small smile, and opened the book to his marker, hoping Elsbeth would take the hint. She didn't.

"I find Merlin to be the most interesting character in the story. He knows what is to come, he leads Arthur toward his destiny and ultimately to his capture by Morgan. He is enigmatic and perhaps the only character who acts from pure selflessness. Don't you agree?"

"I've never cared much for Merlin, or even the magic in the story. It's more about whether our future is fated or if Arthur could have left the sword and chosen the other path. That is what interests me, anyway." Arty pulled the book up closer to his face with another nod, and that seemed to be the signal Elsbeth needed. They rode along in silence, with a few murmurs from the other riders breaking the quiet.

"WE'RE HERE. Make sure you gather your things, I don't want lost items on my bus." The driver said, turning the lever to open the bi-fold door. The riders shuffled off into the late afternoon light, looking up at the large sign of a sword protruding from a stone. They'd arrived at the village of Tintagel and a pub predictably called The Sword in the Stone.

"I'll bring your luggage to the hotel next door. Go in and get yourselves some food. I recommend the bangers and mash, but they make a nice mutton as well. I've heard the curry is quite good also, but that's a bit too spicy for me. Shake a leg now." The driver waved them off, and they headed toward the pub door in clumps of twos and threes. Elsbeth was following in the rear with Arty.

Inside, it was dark wood, smoke, and the smell of old beer. The ceiling was low and the tables close together, gathered around a fire roaring in the back of the room. Large pints of beer were waiting on a long table.

"You're the students from University, yes? Here to work at Tintagel? Welcome." A woman came from behind the bar, wearing a fuzzy teal sweater. Her nose looked red as if it were chapped. Over in the corner, another woman, with dark hair that went down to her waist, sat with a child with orange-red hair. Otherwise, the pub was empty.

"Mr. Dyer will be back after he takes your bags to the hotel. I have some beers waiting for you. Anything stronger than beer is on you to buy; your meal and a beer are included in your per diem." She waved them toward the table, and they each found a spot at the long rectangle. Someone piped up that it should have been a great round table, in keeping with the pub name.

"Why don't you introduce yourselves while I get some plates going." The pub lady had decided she was their de facto host while Mr. Dyer was away.

The travelers took their turns introducing themselves, and the lady was back with platters of roast pork, sausages, steamed cabbage, mashed potatoes, and creamed peas.

"Tuck in because they will work the legs off you up at the site. You'll need your strength." She deposited the platters, then left them to our own devices. It was family-style eating, enough for twice as many mouths as were seated at the table.

"Thank you, this looks lovely." A young woman at the other end of the table said. Arty thought she had said that her name was Porsche, but he couldn't be sure. She had a quiet voice, and it hadn't entirely made it down to his end of the table.

"Eat up, that's good Cornish food there. Are you ready to find treasure, then?" The pub lady smiled as she wiped some glasses by the bar, nodding a greeting as Mr. Dyer came in.

"I doubt there is a treasure to find, but we hope, or at least I hope, to help find discoveries that explore the time of the castle before the Norman conquest, during the time of the Arthur legend," Porsche replied, spearing a sausage from the nearest platter. Arty wished she was sitting closer so he could hear her better.

"Oh, so you think Arthur was just a legend, do you?" Mr. Dyer said, taking a beer from the pub lady. He gave it a deep drink, wiping the foam with the back of his hand.

"Of course. He was just a legend, a folk hero for the native Britons, who were conquered by the Normans and their culture transplanted." Porsche replied, looking at the rest of the table for support. Heads were nodding, but no one chimed in.

"That's your first mistake, girl. Arthur was real. He might not be the Arthur of the legends, but he was real enough. They were all real - Igraine, Uther, even Merlin. Real as you are sitting there." He took another swallow and gave the lady a sly look. *Pulling the legs of gullible students must be his hobby, Arty thought.* He noticed that the dark-haired woman and the young girl were listening.

"Sir, I know it helps the economy here to say so, but Arthur and the Tintagel legend aren't real. I think it takes away from the things that actually happened here, the history and our ancestors who fought first against the Saxons from Wessex and Mercia, and then the invading Normans later on." Porsche sounded a bit louder now, clearly passionate about the topic. A few more voices started to chime in with support.

"Say what you will, girl. But I know what I know. I know what I've seen. That place isn't just a fairy tale ruins for you to dig around. There is magic in the very soil there. Wait and see."

CHAPTER FOUR

"Mum, when are you going to talk with him?" The child with the orange-red hair walked next to her mother as they left the pub, side by side, on the road back toward the castle ruins.

"When the time is right, Lowen," the short, dark-haired woman replied.

"Do you think he'll agree?"

"Yes, I think he will if he understands why we need him."

The pair walked on for a few more moments in silence as a car passed them, giving them a wide berth.

"Mum," Lowen asked, "*why* do we need him, though? I could just go back and save Igraine. Why does it have to be *him*?"

Morgan sighed, having explained this to her daughter once before. Sometimes, Lowen only heard what she wanted to hear.

"Lowen, we need Arty to go back to Tintagel's past because the prophecy says only a child of the dragon can save Igraine. You are many things, my darling daughter, but you are not a child of the dragon." She ruffled the girl's hair, causing Lowen to frown. Eventually, her daughter would be taller than she, but she could still run her fingers through the mop of hair for now.

"Prophecies are stupid. I don't believe in them. Just a bunch of superstition." Lowen's round face was a perfect pout. *She had her grandfather's stubborn streak, Morgan thought.*

"Let's get back to the cottage. I need to prepare a little spell to make sure Arty finds us tomorrow, and you need a bath." Lowen's pout turned into a scowl. She hated bathtime.

"I'll make you a deal, Lowen. You take your bath, and when you are done, I'll let you read some of your grandfather's spell book." The scowl was instantly a wide smile.

"Deal. Let's go." Lowen raced ahead of her mother, her long legs running along the asphalt. She took after her father, long and lean.

With her daughter well ahead of her on the road, Morgan had time to think in peace. It was all so complicated, but it boiled down to one fact. Morgan had made a mess of things, and she needed Arty Drake to help untangle it all. That is what came from meddling with time, of trying to change things fated to be. She'd spent so many years trying to do things on her own, never trusting another, and now she had to bring in a stranger to help set things right. It was a right mess.

"Lowen, slow down. Stay where I can see you." Morgan called to her daughter, but the imp ran faster, heading back toward their little cottage in the hills by the castle ruins. *What did she expect?* She had too much of Morgan in her, and Merlin, truth be told. And her father.

"That child will be the death of me," Morgan muttered as she quickened her pace.

BACK AT THEIR COTTAGE, Morgan flopped into her favorite chair, exhausted from the walk. She wasn't the young girl she had been once. Her mother's blood might keep her from aging as a human woman, but time still played its part in wearing her down. All the tinctures and herbal wraps and muttered spells couldn't stop time's wear. Her fingers ached now in the mornings, and she felt her left knee warn her when cold weather was coming. Age brought wisdom, but it also brought pain.

"I'm done," Lowen hollered from the tiny bathroom, and Morgan heard her splash out of the tub.

"Did you wash your hair?" Morgan called back. Lowen didn't answer, but she heard another splash as the girl climbed back in the tub. She chuckled and reached for the hot tea at her elbow. In a few more minutes, her daughter would be wrapped in a robe and ready to pour over her grandfather's scribbles from thirteen hundred years ago.

Merlin. She tried not to think about him, but it was impossible to keep him totally from her thoughts, especially now, with Arty Drake here. So many painful memories cut at Morgan's mind whenever she thought of her father. He had done such terrible things. He had also tried mightily to redeem himself. Did his regrets and amends balance the scale? She didn't know. She also had done terrible things and she too tried to make amends. *Would Lowen judge her as she judged him?* She shook her head to push the thoughts away. Too painful.

"Alright, Mum, I'm done," Lowen said, padding out to the small living room, wrapped in her mother's robe. Her hair dripped down onto the terry cloth.

"As promised, Merlin's spell book. Don't get it wet! The ink is hard enough to read as it is." Morgan gestured toward the book she had placed in the small chair for Lowen. The cover was a dark brown calf's skin, cracked and scuffed. She remembered when it looked brand new.

"What was he like?" Lowen wiped her hands on her robe before picking up the book. Instead of sitting in the chair, she plopped cross-legged on the wooden floor and opened the book on her lap.

"Complicated. Serious. Proud." Morgan said, keeping the rest of the adjectives to herself.

"I want to meet him, to go back and visit him." Lowen's small fingers traced along the edge of the vellum.

"You know why we can't do that. Every trip back changes the future. Especially with Merlin, we can't change things. We're in enough of a mess as it is, Lowen. Maybe someday, but not now. You promised me." Morgan trusted that her daughter feared her enough to obey, but how much longer would that last. Lowen was head-strong and always knew best.

"I know, Mum. I still wish I could meet him."

"You are more like him than you know. Now hush and read your book. We have a big day tomorrow, so you will have to go to bed early."

CHAPTER FIVE

684 - THE GREAT HALL - CASTLE TINTAGEL

Igraine and Gisela entered the hall to a blaze of torches and a roar of voices. Platters of fish and jugs of ales and wines covered the tables. The courtiers were dressed for the occasion and, near the front of the hall, stood the crew of *The Gloria*.

"Easy to spot, aren't they?" Gisela remarked as Igraine eased her way toward the front and her place at the king's table. She was right about that; their lack of finery wasn't the only reason they were easy to see among the glittering courtiers. The crew had the wind-burned faces and worn hands of people who worked in the sun, not writing poetry or embroidering hemlines. Their faces were full of stories, their eyes brimmed with sights that the court had never seen. Igraine envied them.

"There's your favorite, talking with the lady pirate." Gisela inclined her head, and Igraine turned to see Arthur and Hereca deep in conversation.

"You never call her by her name. Why is that?"

"Because she frightens me. With that strange pointed head of hers and those eyes rimmed in charcoal or whatever she uses. I'd say she is some kind of demon." Igraine could barely hear Gisela's words, she said them so softly, as if Hereca could listen to her over the din of the room. Igraine had to admit; the pirate's appearance did give people pause.

"She's not a demon. She is personable, once you get to know her. She doesn't share much about her life, though. It has taken me almost a year to learn that she was born near the Black Sea, that she was pledged as a bride to a prince of Bavaria, and she escaped to Constantinople. She's been on the seas ever since." They drew closer to the pair, and Gisela fell back behind Igraine.

"Greetings, Arthur, Hereca. Good to see you both." Igraine said, nodding a greeting to them. Arthur smiled, and Hereca nodded in return.

"Your father does like to celebrate when the trade ship returns. It is nice to be considered worthy of invitation at least one day every three months or so." Arthur raised his tankard to his lopsided grin.

"You wear the brooch," Hereca said, a statement of fact with no question to it. Her voice had a marbled sound, edges worn away from all the places she had traveled. Igraine kept her eyes focused on the pirate's face to avoid glancing at her head's elongated crown.

"Yes, it is lovely. Arthur says you are the one I should thank for it. I would love to hear how you acquired it." Igraine had no idea if she would tell her or not.

"I stole it," she said unblinkingly.

"Oh, well, that wasn't quite the story I was expecting, but where did you find it?" The fact that Igraine was wearing a stolen brooch from a city a world away gave her a little shiver of excitement up her spine. Someone far away was missing this treasure, and she would never know them.

"A rich lady, she had many jewels. This one, though, it is from my people, from the days of Atila. His wife, Kreka, was said to have a jeweled bird made of garnets, so I took it." She turned away and walked toward the bench where the rest of the crew was settling in. That was more information than Igraine could have hoped for from Hereca.

"After the meal, will you take a walk with me? You said you wanted to hear about the journey." Arthur said, giving her sleeve a discreet tug before he walked toward his seat. Igraine nodded in reply and turned toward the king's table, where Merlin's eyes greeted her in a beady stare. The old man missed nothing.

As always, the feast began with a blessing to Mor, goddess of the sea, for bringing the travelers safely home. *The Gloria* was the only link to the world outside the Veil; the kingdom traded tin from the mines for spices, oil, wine, and the luxuries of soap, perfume, and fine linen. Only *The Gloria* had the enchantment to pass through the Veil from the sea to bring the treasures home.

"We celebrate another successful return, with the ship ladened to the deck rails thanks to the crew. We give thanks and ask the Dagda to bless you with the strength to continue your journeys for the Kingdom of Dumnonia for many years to come." The king raised his tankard and signaled that all should drink to the crew. The courtiers duly complied, and, with that, the formality of the meal was over. It was time to feast and drink through the night.

"You seem enamored with the sailor, Lady. I do not need to remind you that your husband-to-be will be here soon." Merlin's breath grazed Igraine's ear as he spoke, leaning in to be sure she heard each word. "Whatever attachment you have for that boy, it ends, by your means or mine."

"Teacher, I do not appreciate the accusation. Arthur is my friend, nothing more. I know my duty better than you." Igraine hadn't even sipped her ale yet, but her cheeks were already flushed. *Who was this old man to accuse me of impropriety and of forgetting my duty, she thought.* She was reminded of it every single day.

"Lady, you may fool yourself, but you do not fool me. I know the truth, and I also know that if you do not put aside this infatuation, your friend will not fare well next time he leaves Tintagel." The sorcerer turned from her to speak with the king, expecting no response. *What response could there be to the threat hanging in the air between them?* Igraine's anger pulsed behind her eyes, pushing tears to hang from her lashes. There, in front of the whole of Tintagel, she was moments away from bursting into tears.

"My Lady, might I suggest you take a sip of your ale," Morgan said, from her left. Igraine felt her squeeze her forearm as it rested on the table. "Do not give him the satisfaction of tears, Igraine," she said in a quiet voice meant only for her.

"No, I will not cry," Igraine muttered, more for herself than for Morgan. She sipped at her ale, flavored with honey and woodruff.

"That's good. Put aside the thoughts and focus on the ale. It's good, isn't it? It is delicious with the mustard sauce on the cod. Try some." Igraine knew Morgan was trying to soothe her, as a mother might with a child on the verge of tears. She let the words flow over her like gentle pats on her back. The dark-haired woman spooned some of the cod on Igraine's plate, coaxing her to try it.

"Morgan, you are kind, thank you. I marvel that a daughter of Merlin can be so different from her father." It was an insult to Morgan's father, but one Igraine hoped she wouldn't hold against her. Instead of defending him, Morgan smiled.

"My father and I are alike in many ways, but I think my mother's blood makes me softer than he. Things are rarely as bad as they seem at first. There is always a path through." She gave Igraine's arm another pat and lifted her ale, clinking the edge of the tankard against Igraine's. The princess brushed the few tears from her lashes with the back of her hand.

ENOUGH ALE HAD BEEN CONSUMED, and enough music played where Igraine calculated that her absence wouldn't be noticed. The bards played and sang, filling the hall with stories from the ancient days, and everyone's mind was on something else. Even Merlin's steely gaze was fixed elsewhere when Igraine slipped from the high table and headed for the door and the night air.

The sea smelled especially strong, carried on a fierce wind that pierced even the thick stone walls. For the first time in two hours, Igraine felt that she could breathe.

"Had enough of the feast, have you?" Arthur chimed as she leaned against the wall, taking in a deep breath.

"Oh yes, enough to last until the next one, which will be too soon," she said, opening her eyes again.

"You mean your wedding feast? That comes soon enough, doesn't it?" His smile slipped, which was as close to a frown as his face ever found.

"Let's not talk about that, shall we? You promised me a tale if I walked with you. And here I am. Let's walk." Igraine turned toward the path leading them to land bridge over to the mainland, down to the cove and *The Gloria.*

"Alright, no talk of future days. Let's talk about the voyage, and I'll fill your head with such stories that will have you awake until dawn." He laughed and caught up with Igraine after only a step or two. The torches along the wall of the turris dimly lit their path.

"So it takes almost forty days to reach Constantinople from here. Did you face any pirates on the way?" Almost every trip brought the ship in contact with rogue ships bent on stealing the cargo, making its way along the busy trade route.

"You mean beyond those already on board? No, no pirates this trip. I know that will be a disappointment to you, My Lady. The danger was not at sea this time unless you count the enormous monster we passed near the Pillars of Hercules. It had dozens of long arms, covered with disks and a sharp beak of some kind. It was feasting on another vessel as we came about and we barely escaped."

"Oh, certainly. No doubt a kraken, conjured by Mor herself to destroy your ship. I don't suppose anyone else saw this creature?" He chuckled at her in the darkness.

"Ask Hereca, she saw it as well. I would have thought you'd trust me a little more than that, My Lady." Igraine knew then that he was kidding; Arthur had never once said she should trust him.

"Fine, a monster it was. And you sailed to Constantinople, loaded with tin and ready for trade. How brave of you all." They turned the corner and headed toward the path across the landbridge. There were only a few torches now, and Igraine feared stepping wrong in the shadows. She would have a hard time explaining a broken ankle.

"Yes, brave and stalwart, we sailed into the harbor and plundered the city's streets while the Captain haggled for the best prices. Hereca stole you a jewel, Aemon lost his virginity at a brothel, and…" At the edge of the bridge, he stopped with the dark space of the ravine on either side of them. Below, the ship looked very small.

"And?" Igraine asked, glad they had paused. She wasn't sure she wanted to walk the narrow path in the darkness, even though she'd crossed the landbridge a thousand times.

"And, all I wanted to do was sail back to Tintagel. Back to see you." Arthur kept his eyes focused ahead toward the night.

"Arthur, I…" She didn't know what to say to that. They had teased each other, even flirted at the edge of what was proper, but Arthur had never said something so bold before. He had the world before him, and all he wanted was to sail back to her.

"I shouldn't speak so; I have no right to say that. Please forgive my impertinence. It is the ale talking. Good night, My Lady." He barely said the words before he bolted away, across the bridge in a hurried stride for the cliffside path to the ship below. Igraine stared after him in the darkness until he faded to black.

CHAPTER SIX

Arthur had kept himself busy since the feast; Igraine had hardly seen him as he carried on some errand or other. The only times they seemed to cross paths was when he visited his mother, Edith, in the kitchens, and Igraine was there in the garden. It had been two weeks of brief hellos and waves from across the courtyard, stables, or the landbridge. They hadn't once spoken of what he had said to her, but Igraine had thought of little else.

"Have you found yourself a grasshopper, Longshanks? Let the poor thing alone." Igraine called to his hastening tail across the herb beds. Edith wouldn't be happy to see her lavender plants trampled by his pouncing paws.

The book in her lap was faded but still legible in the late morning light. The vellum pages stiff under her fingers, with the symbols and words written in dark red ink. Vines threaded around the edges of the page, their ink a pearlescent green. In among the greenery, the illuminator had added dark emerald thorns.

"*Gwau'r llen, tynnu i lawr ar y tir. Tu ôl i thiced, ar goll i'r cof. Warchod y tir a'i phobl,*" Igraine whispered, tracing the symbols on the vellum. The ink seemed to pulsate beneath the pad of her finger as she drew the sigils. This was just practice - no ritual or purification, no sacrifice given. Still, Igraine couldn't imagine the power of drawing down a Veil to guard the entire kingdom, to protect everyone she had ever loved. It was almost beyond her reason to think that she had a part to play in whether her people lived or died.

Weave the Veil, drawn down upon the land. Behind a thicket, lost to memory. Guard the land and her people.

"Igraine, are you there?" Igraine heard Morgan's call from the kitchen doorway. She rarely came to the garden to intrude on her time.

"Yes, Morgan. I'm here," Igraine called back, rising from her wooden bench.

"He's here, Igraine. The Pendragon delegation is here, and Uther is with them." Words Igraine had dreaded hearing for a fortnight now spoken, hanging heavy over the salad greens. She clutched the book of magic against her chest and walked toward Morgan. It was happening.

"I suspect my father will wish to see me, to have me greet the guests." Igraine stepped into the shadows of the kitchen, leaving the warm light behind her.

"I should think so. I thought you ought to know." Morgan gave her a slight hug and headed back along the narrow corridor, back to Merlin. Edith came into the room, loaded with a large basket of spring cabbages.

"Why so gloomy on a glorious day, Lady? You aren't feeling faint, are you? I could make you a tisane if you are feeling poorly." She set the basket down with a thump to place a hand on the young woman's forehead.

"I have no fever, Edith. I am well, truly. How goes your errant son? I haven't seen much of him these days." She continued to press her moist palm against Igraine's forehead, unaware of how strange that might look, a cook's hand on a princess's brow.

"Busy as a *bucca* in the mines and twice as ornery. He's hardly had a good word for his mother since he returned from the voyage. And now he tells me, he is taking off again, having convinced the captain to make a short run to Brittany. He says he may be gone for a bit, to seek his fortune on land for a time. Breaks his mother's heart, he does." She chattered on, finally lowering her palm from Igraine's forehead and resuming her inspection of her cabbages. The scullery maids came along to help with the midday meal, and Igraine used the distraction to make her exit.

She barged through the passages, heading out into the light of the stable yard nearby. Pendragon horses were fed and watered as their attending pages saw to their needs. The red dragon against the dark blue of their livery caught her eye.

"Quite a spectacle, no?" Arthur said, leaning against the wall nearby. He always seemed to be doing that.

"Here to see your mother?" Igraine asked, her tone cold and waspish.

"Here to see you. I suppose she has told you then, by the sound of your voice." He was chewing thoughtfully on a piece of dried meat, the rations of a sailor.

"Yes, she mentioned that you are heading to Brittany and then lands unknown."

"We'll set sail soon as we are stocked up again. It won't be a long trip, but yes, I am likely going to stay awhile ashore, once we land." He paused again to chew on the strip of meat.

"Your mother will miss you, you know. She says you are breaking her heart." Igraine took a step closer to him.

"I know, but it won't be forever. Just for now." He leaned away from the wall, standing straight before turning squarely toward her. "My Lady, this is something I must do. I know it doesn't please you, but you will be gone from Tintagel soon enough, and I don't want to be here when you leave this place. You've been a fixture here as long as I have. It won't be home without you here." He tossed the remnant of the meat onto the ground.

Igraine's mind whirled for a response. She had no idea what he expected her to say to him. Surely, he knew the last thing she wanted was to leave Tintagel, leave her friends, her father, and everything she had known for the previous eighteen years. She had never set foot out of their lands, and now she would be leaving them forever.

"Nothing to say to that? As you wish." He turned to leave, but

Igraine grabbed his gray tunic sleeve to hold him. It was rough under her fingers, nothing more than befitting a sailor.

"Arthur, don't do this. Don't leave yet. There is so little time left to us, let us share the last of these days together. Please, don't leave for Brittany, not yet." Igraine was pleading. She'd never spoken that way to him, never been serious with him about anything. They had laughed and played and teased all the time they had known each other since they were children.

"Igraine." He said her name as if he had never said it before; he always called her "Lady". "What you ask of me, if you only knew, is more than anyone should have to bear. But because you ask it, I will try." Her hand crept along the fabric until she found the solid arm beneath it, and she squeezed it. He felt so solid, an anchor holding her in place.

"I cannot do my duty if I don't have you here. It may be weak of me to ask you, but I need to know you are here with me. I know it is more than I have a right to expect, but…"

"Enough. Say no more. I'll stay, Lady. Until you pass along the landbridge with your bridegroom at your side, I will stay." With a soft pull, his arm left her grip, and he walked away, back toward the Pendragon pages brushing their horses in the warm June sun.

♛

"Lady Igraine, may I present the Prince of Ceredigion, Uther of the clan of Pendragon." Merlin made the introduction as Igraine stood before the king, and the tall stranger still dressed for the road. His sandy blond hair was matted from sweat. Not the ideal meeting of one's betrothed.

"My Lady, I would take your hand in greeting, but I fear the scent of my horse might be more than you could bear. I am in need of refreshing after the ride, but I wanted to meet you straight away." He finished with a short bow of courtesy, dipping his head ever so slightly.

"Prince Uther, it is good that you have arrived safely from your journey. I greet you warmly and extend the hospitality of Tintagel to you and your party." If she could have replied with more formality, she wasn't sure how she could have done it. This was no friend Igraine was greeting; this was the man she was forced to marry. The king raised an eyebrow at her but said nothing.

"I accept your hospitality for myself and the good men of Ceredigion who accompanied me here. I look forward to spending time here in Tintagel and learning more about the lady who has called this castle home." Uther took her lead and slid into formality as well; no more talk of horse scent for this prince.

"There will be time for that, surely, Uther, but for now, I wish to hear of the actions of Mercia and their invasions into your lands. Have you kept them from gaining hold in the east?" Her father leaned toward Uther as if his failing eyesight meant he couldn't hear him as well. Igraine knew better than to assume she had been dismissed.

"Mercia gains in strength, sending men to invade along our shared border, but thank the Morrigan, we have been able to repel their advance. Word among the men is they have a spellcaster that has joined their ranks. Knowing Æthelred's reputation as a man of Christianity, I cannot believe that is so, but perhaps someone in his kingdom works without his knowledge. Without the promise of the Veil, I don't know how long we will be able to keep them at bay." Uther finished, glancing at Igraine with his final words. *Yes, the promise of the Veil. The reason for this marriage,* she thought.

"Soon enough, the Veil will draw down upon Ceredigion as it has over Dumnonia, and your enemies will forget why they ever came to your lands in the first place. Your kingdom will fade from memory, just as ours has for the last five years. Peace amongst our peoples," the king said as if speaking to an audience of courtiers and not just the three of them. He always had a flair for the dramatic.

"Might I beg your leave, King Geraint, and pause our discussions so that I might refresh from the journey?" A host used to visitors might have made that offer earlier, but Tintagel hadn't received formal visitors in over five years, so perhaps the king could be forgiven for forgetting this. Geraint waved his hand at Uther.

"Oh, yes, of course. I have forgotten my manners it seems. Yes, please refresh yourself and then join us for the midday meal. We can discuss matters later. My page will show you to your chambers." From the side of the hall, Simon, his page of many years, melted from the shadows and appeared next to the prince. With a deep bow, he turned and led Uther toward the doors.

"Until later, Lady Igraine. We will have much to speak of."

Igraine watched him leave, catching the scent of a horse just as he had feared. *What could she know of this stranger after only a few words, she thought.* She had much to learn about Uther Pendragon and there was hardly any time left.

CHAPTER SEVEN

"Arthur, are you going to help us prepare, or are you going to mope for your princess?" Hereca's words scattered his thoughts, and Arthur jolted his head to look at her. The indomitable pirate had her hands on her hips and her lips pursed in disgust.

"Right, sorry. I lost track of time. I was in my thoughts." Arthur rose from his rope pile seat and reached for a box to haul below deck. He'd been lost in his thoughts ever since coming back to Tintagel.

"I know she is pretty and all, but let's be honest, pretty girls aren't hard to find. She can't be that good in bed that you've lost your senses." A smudge of a smile now bent Hereca's pursed lips, and Arthur had to smile himself, though he should be outraged by the suggestion.

"Do not sully the honor of the Lady Igraine, Hereca. She is my friend, that is all. And yes, I have no trouble finding pretty women at our ports of call, thank you kindly. But Igraine…" How could he explain to Hereca something he didn't understand himself. His childhood friend and companion, the girl he had raced around the castle paths, and usually lost to, was leaving his world. His friend, who was more than a friend but only in his mind, never in reality.

"But you love her," Hereca said, grabbing a box of her own to take below and stack with the others. The rogues around them were giving them scalding looks for standing idle.

"Care to help?" Aemon said, giving Arthur's arm a sharp nudge with his own.

Hereca spat at him before replying, "Take care, Aemon, or your virginity won't be the only thing now lost to you. You might be ready for the eunuchs' choir in Byzantium soon if you don't take care." Aemon laughed in response but stayed outside of Hereca's reach.

"Love Igraine? What makes you say that?" Arthur carried his load to the small steps leading below deck, where he'd hand the crate off to a crewman to stack. The hold smelled like fish and olive oil from the last voyage.

"I say nothing, Arthur. Your face says everything. If you love her, tell her. Don't wait for some miracle to bring her to you. Be bold or stop moping. Your choice." He felt the box she carried nudge him in the back as she followed him down the stairs. Everything was so black and white with Hereca. It was all so easy.

"You don't understand," he replied, passing off his box and then turning to take Hereca's from her. The pair then retreated to the top deck to grab another set.

"And you don't think. You love her, but you do nothing. If you love her and do nothing, then you deserve nothing. Isn't this girl worth fighting for? If she is not, then find another. It isn't that complicated."

"Why am I talking to you about this?" Arthur said, annoyed that she was boiling down his situation to something easy to say but impossible to do.

"Because no one else will listen to you. And now I am done listening as well. You either make your move, or you move on. Let's have no more moon-eyed gazing from you, Arthur Spear. I've seen you fight, I've seen you steal, I've seen you save your friends and slay your enemies. Now fight for your woman."

Before Arthur could respond, the pirate walked from him, down the plank to the beach, where more supplies waited for carting aboard. If he had held a stone, he might have thrown it at her. She could be infuriating. She was also right.

"Damn it, I should have stayed in Carthage," he said to no one, hoisting another box to hand to Aemon below deck.

♛

"Father, I must speak with you," Morgan said, entering Merlin's study. The candles flickered in the breeze of her wake.

"What is it, Morgan?" He replied, keeping his eyes fixed on the parchment on the table. How anyone could look so old and yet also ageless was beyond her. But then, her father's blood held many secrets. He was mortal, but he came from a long line of spellcasters.

"It's about Igraine and the union. Father, I think we are making a mistake." She crossed over to the bench near the table and sat next to him, folding her hands in her lap. It was several seconds before he looked up.

"What makes you say that, Morgan?"

"What you ask of her is too much. It should not be her burden to bear. This union is not what she wants. You know that. It isn't what Uther Pendragon wants either, truth be told. There must be another way to protect the Veil, surely, without destroying the lives of two innocent people."

Merlin put his quill down and folded his fingers, interlacing them atop the parchment. His gray eyes were buried under long strands of white eyebrows.

"Morgan, you know as well as I that the Veil will not hold if a sacrifice is not made. It must be a sacrifice from one of the blood of this kingdom. She must join with Pendragon, and she must produce the one who will seal the Veil for good. The fact that she, and you, find this distasteful changes nothing. Do not let your emotions get the better of you, Morgan. You know the prophecy as well as I."

She had known this would be his response. Duty was more important than anything else. Responsibility at any price. Except, he never seemed to be the one paying that price - always someone else.

"Father, we don't know for certain that the prophecy is true. We don't know for certain that the Veil will fall if such a sacrifice is not made. We are making these choices, and yet we don't know whether any of this is true. Surely, your sorcery can protect the people of Dumnonia without all this." Morgan waved, as if the Veil were right there, cloaking them under its tangle of shrouded magical vines and thorns.

"I know well enough that the kingdoms that have the Veil in place - kingdoms such as Baltia, the Isle of Amber, Atlantis of the Greeks, and Zerzura, the desert city of little birds - they all live in protection, faded from memory into legend. Their rulers made the sacrifice necessary to save their people. Those that have not, such as the king of Babylon, fell to their fate. Would you have Dumnonia fall as well so a girl can love a sailor?" He unclasped his hands and reached for his quill. Apparently, there was nothing left to say.

"I do not believe that it is your place or my place or even the king's place to decide for Igraine what is best for her, to take her free will away to fulfill some prophecy. At least tell her what is to come, let her decide her own fate. Can you not give her that?"

"Morgan, enough of this. She has her part to play in this, and nothing changes that. I forbid you from discussing this further. Nothing must interfere, not even my daughter. Are we understood? The Veil grows weaker by the day." His eyes were now the color of dark slate. Her father was a terrible force when he was angry.

"I understand, Father. I don't agree. But I understand." She rose from the bench, and with a curt nod of her head, she left him to his parchment, walking back into the rosy June sunshine.

Across the castle, Igraine sat in her garden, studying a book to learn magic that she would never need. She didn't know that the magic was in her blood, in her womb, not the words she had studied for years, the lies she had been told - the lies Morgan and Merlin had told her to keep her compliant. She didn't know that her sacrifice was nothing less than her own child yet to be conceived. Merlin had tricked Igraine into believing her magic skills would save her world. And Morgan had helped with that trick.

She walked toward the landbridge to look over at the moored ship where Igraine's true love was preparing for another journey. The galley bobbed on the water as the anchor held it fast to the cove. Along the cliff's edge, she spied a small sylph, a tiny air fairy, hovering as Morgan leaned to pick a little flower.

"Greetings, cousin," the sylph said. Fae creatures could always tell another fae. Anyone else in the castle grounds wouldn't have seen the air spirit at all.

"Greetings. What brings you here?" Morgan asked, curious to see the creature in the broad light of midday. Sylphs preferred glens and dales rather than the crags of the coastline.

"I am gathering blossoms for my supper, and these looked especially tasty. Besides, there is such magic radiating here on this land, how could I not be drawn here. Powerful magic indeed, even within the Veil. It is intoxicating, like the best elderberry wine." The sylph floated up toward where Morgan stood and hovered near her face. She could see the land and the sky through her opaque form.

"No doubt that is my father, Merlin. He is the greatest sorcerer, and magic follows in his wake." The sylph crinkled up her nose as if sniffing something very hard, trying to draw every drop of scent from the wind.

"Yes, we know of Merlin, and yes, I smell his power. I smell yours as well. But there is something else. Magic that is raw like honey and unfinished, but there on the wind. There is another here who wields power, a power that lies sleeping. Can you not tell, daughter of *aes sidhe*?" The sylph began to float away, spying another posey for her collection. With a buffet of sea wind, she was gone.

It had to be Igraine - none other had the magic. Magic that was raw like honey and unfinished? It must be the magic of her bloodline, untapped, and untested. But was it powerful enough that the sylph could sense it on the wind? How was that possible, Morgan wondered. Igraine came from magic blood, but she was no sorceress.

"What does any of this mean?" she asked the wind. "Can we really defend this kingdom with a lie?" The wind said nothing in return.

CHAPTER EIGHT

1984 - FIRST DAY AT THE RUINS OF CASTLE TINTAGEL

There wasn't a cloud in the blazing blue sky as the bus brought the students to the ruins of the castle. They trooped off the bus with backpacks loaded for the day. Day one was orientation, spending the day exploring the ruins, meeting the staff, and learning about the discoveries already found at the site where the legendary King Arthur came into the world. Arty could hardly wait.

"And the game is afoot," Elsbeth said, stepping from the bus behind him. Her backpack probably weighed more than she did.

"Yes, it is. It should be an amazing experience." Arty replied as he followed Mr. Dyer up the slope toward the long buildings at the parking lot's end. Rolling green stretched all around, with not a tree in sight.

Mr. Dyer shook hands with a short, stout lady near the building, who would need high heels to reach five feet tall. She wore a long crocheted sweater vest in a shade of caramel brown, reaching the hem of her black polyester slacks.

"Ladies and gents, please meet Dr. O'Malley, your boss for the rest of your time at Tintagel. Listen to the good lady now. She's been with the site for many years and knows all of its secrets." Mr. Dyer swept off his gray cap and gave a flourished bow, to which the doctor curtsied. Porsche chuckled from behind the group.

"Greetings, students. Welcome to Tintagel! We are pleased to have you here. We will work you to the bone, we won't pay you, and you will remember this as the best experience of your life. Come inside and let's get acquainted with the site." Dr. O'Malley turned on her heel and led them into the gray building while Mr. Dyer pulled out a cigarette package, waving them along as they went.

"Gather around, we'll go over the history of the site, from the Roman occupation to the High Middle Ages to the tourist trade of the 19th century. And yes, we'll even talk about good old King Arthur. There have been focused archaeological excavations ongoing here since the 1930s."

The students settled in, and Dr. O'Malley began her lecture. Arty knew most of it already. By the year 1233, the site was already famous as Arthur's birthplace, so the first Duke of Cornwall decided to cash in on that legend and build a castle there. Arty wasn't surprised to hear the doctor share that scholars claimed none of the castle ruins were from Arthur's time, though others in his cohort seemed to be. The only structures from the 600s looked to be squat stone buildings with thatched roofs; hardly the high stone walls of fortified castles. *Why wasn't there any archaeological evidence for an early Tintagel castle, Arty wondered, if the legends all said it was there?*

"Isn't it fascinating?" Elsbeth elbowed him, whispering loudly enough for most of the group to hear. Arty nodded in reply.

"Now that you know the basic history, we'll go over the types of items we have found recently and the area of the site where you will be stationed. You'll want to take some notes."

♛

DR. O'MALLEY KEPT up her speech for several hours, and by lunchtime, Arty was ready for a break. No matter how fascinating a subject matter, the human mind can only stay attentive for so long. He found his thoughts drifting as she spoke toward the end. *Why had the story of Arthur taken root in the place? Of all of Britain, why this corner of the world?*

"Let's take a break for some nosh, shall we?" Dr. O'Malley gestured toward the door, and with a collective murmur, the group rose.

Arty was glad to get back outside into the sunshine, and he stretched mightily, reaching for both his toes and then the blue sky. Twisting from side to side, he was anxious to move.

"Aren't you coming over for luncheon?" Elsbeth asked, signaling toward the table with sack lunches.

"Can you do me a favor and grab one for me? I'm going to take a quick walk to stretch my legs. I'll be back soon." Before Elsbeth could offer to join him, Arty gave her a wave and sprinted toward a green hill.

Nothing smells as good as sea air, whether that sea is off the coast of Seattle or Tintagel. He drew in a big breath and pounded his feet on the parking slab toward the earth mound. There would be many days ahead of squatting in the dirt, barely moving to avoid injury to the dig site.

Arty reached the mound in no time, seeing a slight path now that he was closer. The trail was a narrow one, hardly sketched into the hill's base, but he slowed his pace and followed it. He expected it to lead around the hill and perhaps a steeper climb to a hillside view of the sea. Instead, rounding the hill, he saw a squat, stone house with a thatched roof tucked into the small cleft. A glorious garden served as the front gate.

"Must be a caretaker's cottage," he muttered out loud, ambling toward the first row of flowers, a growing shelter against the sea winds.

"You're finally here. Mum's been waiting," a girl said, poking her head out from a stand of peonies. Her carrot-orange hair was long, and her eyes seemed almost too big for her face. She couldn't have been more than ten years old.

"Excuse me? Hello, is your mother expecting me as part of the excavation project?" Arty imagined she was Dr. O'Malley's daughter, although the good doctor seemed a bit too old for a daughter this age.

"You should follow me," she said, stepping out to a series of flagstones that led through the garden's tangle. Her orange head bobbed along toward the front door of the cottage.

"Wait! I don't think your mom is expecting me.' This had to be some mistake, and he wasn't keen on following some child into her house.

She didn't turn to look but instead opened the green front door and went inside, leaving him alone in the garden.

Arty had no idea what to do. Should he follow the girl and knock on the door or turn around and head back toward the meeting building and his sack lunch? A few moments passed before the orange head poked out and she looked at him with those large eyes.

"Are you coming or not? The tea is ready."

He stepped on the flagstone and toward the strange child's invitation to tea.

The ceiling of the cottage was low, and the beams almost black with age. Arty had to remind himself to duck as he crossed the threshold and examined the open room. Stacks of books lined the walls, serving as some kind of moat around the room. A fireplace with a cheery flame heated the place, and a table to his left held a squat, brown teapot, a tray of small sandwiches, and some scones.

"Take a seat, she's just washing up," the girl said, pouring tea from the pot into three cups. A small pitcher of cream and a plate of lemons completed the scene.

"I'm not sure who your mother is, but I think you've made a mistake. I'm Arty Drake, I'm a student here for my semester archaeology dig project." He hoped that would have cleared it up, but instead, she nodded sagely and added a lump of sugar to her cup.

"Yep, we know," she said before giving the cup a swirl with a small silver spoon. There was nothing else to say but to wait for her mother to solve this mystery.

Arty heard a noise off the main room before a door opened and a woman appeared, with dark hair braided and coiled on top of her head.

She wore a loose blouse, the color of blood, and linen trousers, and her feet were bare. She couldn't have been much more than five feet tall.

"Mum, he's here," the girl said, by way of introduction, taking another sip from her cup. Arty hadn't moved from his spot at the door.

"Well, and so he is. Greetings, we are glad you are here. Please come in, take some tea with us. You must be wondering what this is all about." The woman gestured toward the table as she crossed over and patted her daughter on the shoulder. Arty knew exactly how Alice in Wonderland felt at the Mad Hatter's tea party.

"Alright," he said, lamely, stepping deeper into this weird place and pulling back a chair from the table. The girl was loading up a plate with sandwiches and scones.

"Let's help set you at ease. My name is Morgan, and this is my daughter, Lowen. And we know that you are Arty - Arthur, actually - from America. We've been waiting for you, and now you are here." She smiled, and two dimples appeared in the cheeks of her round face.

"Why were you waiting for me? Do you work with Dr. O'Malley?" He took the plate the girl offered and placed it lightly on the table. He wasn't so sure he should eat or drink anything in here if he played the part of Alice.

"No, though we've known of the doctor since she was a student here. No, we aren't part of the project site. This is our home and has been for...well a long, long time." She smiled again and poured cream into her tea.

"Then I don't understand, how do you know me?"

"I know you are confused, and what I am going to tell you will sound insane, I know. But please, hear me out. I promise it will all make sense eventually. Arthur - Arty, sorry - we have been waiting for you because you come from a special family. A family that has its roots right here in Tintagel."

"I'm not sure what you mean. My Mom's family is from Norway originally, and yes, my Dad's family is from Britain but not in Cornwall." The girl gave her mother a look he couldn't interpret.

"Mum, just tell him. Skirting around it isn't working."

With a sigh, her mother nodded. "Yes, Lowen, I suppose there is no easy way to say this, so I'll just lay it out for him." She put down her cup and placed both hands on the table as if bracing herself. "Arty, you are the descendant of Arthur, King of Britons. King Arthur was real. He was born here, at Tintagel, and you are of his bloodline."

Arty couldn't have been more surprised if she had confirmed he was in fact, in Wonderland. He stared at her face, looking for the signs that she was joking, but there was nothing there but complete earnestness. Lowen was nodding next to her.

"That's not all, Mum. Tell him everything."

"Lowen, please. Let me handle things. He needs time to take in all the information. These things can't be rushed." Morgan said, in a voice you might use with an adult, not a precocious ten-year-old.

"So, you are saying my father's family line begins with Arthur, *the* Arthur, and that I am his descendant? How do you know this?"

Morgan had picked up her cup and taken a quick sip before setting it down again. Lowen was munching happily on a scone, covering the lace tablecloth with tiny currants and crumbs.

"Arty, because I was there."

He didn't mean to knock the chair over when he stood, but the force carried it over, and it crashed against the stone floor. He almost hit his head against the overhead beam in the process.

"Don't leave yet. Just hear me out. As I told you, this will all make sense. You need to hear me out, though." Morgan's voice sounded like she was trying to soothe a colicky baby.

"No, I think I have heard quite enough, thank you. I'm not sure what game you and your kid are playing at, but I don't appreciate it. Bad enough to float some crazy idea that I'm King Arthur's great great great times ten grandkid, but then you are also a time traveler? Yeah, that was a bridge too far, I'm afraid." He walked over toward the door, and Lowen started laughing.

"Told you he wouldn't believe it, Mum. He has to see it." Arty stopped, hand on the doorknob. *He has to see it? See what, he wondered.*

"Arty, please sit back down, I will tell you everything, and maybe Lowen is right, maybe I have to show you. But please, give me a chance." He looked back over his shoulder to the woman standing at the table, hand reaching toward him.

"Look, I think this is crazy, alright? But if you have some kind of proof, as you say, then show me."

"Yes, I can prove it to you, I can, but first you must let me tell you everything and then you can decide if you want to see for yourself. Deal?" His hand slipped from the doorknob. *Why in the world was he listening to this woman, he wondered.*

"Alright. I'll listen to everything. Spill it." He wasn't going to move from his spot by the door, though.

"My name is Morgan, as I told you. I am the daughter of Merlin, the sorcerer. I was born hundreds of years before Arthur, though I don't know precisely when. My father never told me. My mother's people were *aes sídhe*, what you might call fairies. It's her blood that gives me my longevity.

"My father and I came to Tintagel when it was the High Seat of the Kingdom of Dumnonia - King Geraint was the ruler. In those days, Britain was not one kingdom; the Romans had left two hundred years before, and warlords were trying to conquer the island. Dumnonia was in threat from the Saxon invaders to the east and Mercia's soldiers from the north. The king knew they would be overrun eventually and the people destroyed. So he agreed to an offer from my father, Merlin.

"Merlin knew how to cast a Veil over the Dumnonia - not a veil that you could see, but something much more powerful. This Veil was magic - think of it as a thicket of vines and thorns that blocks the way from anyone remembering that Dumnonia was ever there. The Veil fogged the invaders' memory, causing them to forget why they ever marched west in the first place. It came from powerful and ancient magic that only a few have mastered. It takes strong magic in the blood to create and then a sacrifice to maintain. My father made the Veil, but Igraine, the king's daughter, would have to provide the sacrifice."

Morgan paused, taking another sip of her tea before sweeping Lowen's crumbs onto her empty plate. She glanced back at Arty, waiting for him to say something. *What in the world could he say in response to that; the woman was clearly crazy, he thought.*

"Because I can move through time, I have watched your family line for hundreds of years, and I have moved into the future to see what is to come. There are great things in store for you, Arty. Great things indeed. But it is the past that I wish to discuss, to save your family's destiny and in truth, the people of Dumnonia."

She had promised to make everything clear, but nothing was clear to him at all. She was a time traveler and the daughter of Merlin. Arty was the descendant of Arthur, and he had to go into the past to save his family and some ancient kingdom. None of it made a lick of sense to him.

"I've heard your story, but it hasn't convinced me that it is true. It sounds crazy, and frankly, I think you are still trying to trick me somehow, or maybe you just need some professional help. Unless you have some kind of proof, I'm going to leave now."

"I'll take him," Lowen said, reaching for another scone. "I'll take him back. That will prove it."

CHAPTER NINE

Igraine had made it through the evening meal, listening to her uncle's new bride, Laria, prattle on and on and on. Never had a bride loved her bridegroom as much as Laria loved Igraine's uncle, Ithyl - known throughout the kingdom as "Ithyl the rock". Nearest she could guess, the nickname honored his stout heart and spine, but Igraine always thought it referenced his head.

"Aren't you excited about your wedding, Igraine? Uther Pendragon is quite the match - a prince and handsome as well. Not as handsome as Ithyl, mind you, but handsome enough, I would wager. You must be over the moon with happiness that an arranged match ends so well. My sister's betrothal to Lord Huwal, well, let's just say, it hasn't fared to her liking. Did you like the fish tonight? That dill sauce was delightful, I would say…"

The one-sided conversation had driven Igraine to take more than her share of ale, and she was feeling the effects. She was so close to telling Laria to close her ever-gaping maw; she had to press her lips together to keep the words at bay. Igraine knew she had to get out of the hall before she did something she would regret.

"Forgive me, Laria, but I must excuse myself. I feel a headache coming on, and I need a tisane of chamomile and mint." Igraine rose, albeit shakily from the drink, from the table and signaled to Gisela, who was dining further down the hall with the court's other ladies. Out of the corner of her eye, Igraine caught the glance of Uther. He was smiling as if he knew exactly what she was doing.

"Oh, you must rest, Igraine, you must. A headache can become quite grave if you aren't careful. My sister lost the vision in her right eye for a fortnight when she let her headache get the best of her. I shall come by your rooms later to tend to you. No, no, I shan't be dissuaded. Go now, and I will come by later." With a shooing motion of her hands, Laria scooted Igraine away from the High Table, and she made her escape.

The darkness was a tonic after the noise and the ruckus of the hall. It settled over her, and Gisela's torch gave them the light they needed to head down the path. It was dark out but not quiet; on the wind, they could hear laughter and shouts.

"What is that about?" Igraine asked Gisela, turning toward the landbridge and the direction of the sound.

"The crew of *The Gloria*, making merry on the beach below. It sounds as if they've had a bit too much to drink as well." Even with the ale addling Igraine's brain, she caught the jab.

"Let's see what they are about," Igraine said, taking a step from the cliffside onto the bridge that was scarcely the width of four people abreast. All the goods needed for the castle came back and forth across this narrow strip of land. *How many trips in a day were made carrying baskets, leading horses, hauling logs for the fire, she wondered.*

"Lady, I do not think it is wise to join their party. Your father would certainly not approve. I think it best we retire to your room." Gisela called after her, and Igraine heard her shuffling behind to catch up.

"Gisela, it harms no one, and you will be with me. They are friends down there, not armed bandits. Well, they *are* armed bandits and pirates, but friends nonetheless. Let's go."

IT TOOK a while to reach the base of the cliffside at the other end of the landbridge. Igraine had to tread carefully down the hewn rock stairs, clutching the rope that strung as a railing. Finally, she reached firm land below, and she heard Gisela sigh loudly behind her. Igraine glanced back to the steep dark stairs and shuddered; they'd have to make their way back up those again.

The beach was tiny round stones, shifting under each footstep. Pebbles rolled and crunched as they made their way to the water's edge. The crew had lit a bonfire, and it blazed merrily against the dark crashing waves. Igraine could make out the sailors' silhouettes against the firelight, and Hereca's pointed head was easy to spot.

"Friends," Igraine called toward them. "We've come to join your party." Heads turned toward them, and a sword unsheathed, followed by a loud "put that away" from Hereca.

"Lady Igraine, what are you doing here," the woman asked, standing up from her log perch. She had a long piece of orange fabric wound around her head, something a woman of Constantinople might wear if Arthur's stories were to be believed.

"I come to see my friends and enjoy the light of your fire. I hope we are welcome." Igraine replied, and her cheeks glowed red but not from the bonfire. *Maybe Gisela had been right after all.*

"Of course you're welcome," Arthur responded, walking from around the fire's edge, his long thin frame outlined by the flame. No wonder his nickname was Spear.

Igraine heard Gisela cluck behind her, but she said nothing. The pair made their way forward, toward the log where Hereca had been sitting. Arthur met them at the edge.

"What are you celebrating?" Igraine asked Hereca as she settled herself onto the log and made room for them.

"We lit a fire to honor the sea gods; we burned some olive oil and some of this strange dried herb we picked up in Carthage. They called it *hashish*, I believe. Anyway, it is good to make an offering before any voyage, no matter what gods you worship."

Arthur took a spot on a stump, facing the log, with his back to the fire. He held a cup in his hand, and he offered it to Igraine. She reached out and took it, taking a sip of his beer before offering it back. Arthur waved it off.

"Hereca, forgive me, I know this question may seem impertinent, but I hope you won't be angry if I ask you...about your head." The words were scarcely out of Igraine's mouth before Gisela gasped next to her.

Arthur exploded in laughter, and Igraine watched in horror as those kohl-rimmed eyes bored into her. *Great Goddess, what have I done?*

"Lady, I am not accustomed to such a bold question, but I will forgive the rudeness because you have been drinking. The ways of my people, the descendants of Atila, may seem strange to you. Those born of the magic blood are, at birth, bound at their skull, signifying their power. I come from a long line of shamans, of wise women and spell guardians. My people are scattered now, and the old ways die out, but there are still a few of us in the world who look like this." She gestured to her skull, and Igraine could picture the infant Hereca with her little head squeezed tightly for months to achieve such a shape. It seemed so cruel.

"Forgive me, Hereca. I meant no offense. But if you are a shaman, why do you sail on this ship?" It seemed impossible that someone born to her fate would be sailing instead on a trading vessel.

"Because I choose to," she said simply, lifting her cup to her lips. "I decide my fate and my fortune." It was all she was going to say on the matter.

"Lady, join me near the shoreline, will you?" Arthur said, standing up and offering her his hand. Igraine heard the start of Gisela's protests, but she shushed her, handing her the cup she held. *Gisela could sit in silence with Hereca and ponder how life had brought her to this place, lady in waiting to a drunk princess on the edge of the sea.*

"Yes, I will," Igraine replied, taking his hand and leaving the bonfire's warmth. The crew had started singing some rowdy song about a selkie, the seal women of the sea, and Igraine heard the sound of a pipe join the melody.

"Igraine, you shouldn't have come down here. Your father will be furious. You know that." Arthur led her forward, keeping clear of the dark water. There was a sliver of moonlight shining on the ripples.

"And what if he is? What will he do? Lock me in my room? I am not afraid of him," Igraine replied, feeling brave with the Lord of Tintagel far above in the feasting hall.

Arthur stopped and turned, holding on to her shoulders now, staring down into her face. "Igraine, why are you here? You know there is nothing to be gained by it. I promised to stay until the...until it was done, but coming here, it is not kind, Igraine."

Igraine took in his words, trying to let them sink in that her very presence was an unkindness to him. *How could he think that?* Friends since childhood and now, a closeness that she felt with no other living soul, was being snuffed out by his words.

"Arthur, I never want to be unkind, never to you. I have only ever been your friend. I came because I wanted to see you. There isn't much time, I know, but I had to see you, and now you say it was unkind..." The tears were coming, streaming down her cheeks, and he reached up to wipe them from her skin. His hand felt rough, long cut by the edges of ropes and swords.

"Igraine, it is unkind because the woman I love, whom I cannot be with, who burns in my every thought, who treads my dreams, is right here next to me, and I cannot have her." His face was inches from hers now.

"I am not his, not yet. I am still Igraine, Lady of Tintagel, and you are Arthur Spear, the man that I love." Igraine leaned toward him and found his lips with her own. He was warm and solid next to her, blocking the wind with his body, shielding her from the sailors' sight as they sang about the mysterious selkie. His hands squeezed her shoulders before he took a step back and broke the spell.

"Say the word, and I will take you from here, we'll sail away and never look back. Just say the word, Igraine. You cannot marry him."

"I must go, I have to get back, but Arthur, promise me you will come find me tomorrow." Igraine took his hand and squeezed it, feeling the roughness again. She never wanted to hold another hand than his.

"I promise, Igraine. I'll find you."

CHAPTER TEN

"Father, do you have a few moments to spare," Igraine asked, peering around the corner where he sat at a small table in his private apartments. She couldn't remember the last time she had visited him there, perhaps, once or twice as a young girl to bring him some posies or some such.

"Daughter, what do you need," he replied, looking up from papers that she knew he could scarcely read. He had the convex glass that Merlin had given him held above the text so it could appear before his dimmed eyes. Igraine suspected in another summer, he would be blind altogether. *Why couldn't his wizard make him see again, she wondered.*

"I want to speak with you about the union, about Uther." Igraine watched him place the glass on the table and turn toward her, settling back in his wooden chair. His face was still handsome, even if his eyes had a milky-white sheen to them.

"What is it?" For once, his voice sounded quiet, as if resignation had taken all the air from him.

"Father, I know my duty is to the kingdom, to you, and to maintaining the Veil, but...I cannot marry Uther. I cannot do as you and Merlin ask; it is too great a burden to place on me, Father." There was no chair near him, and she wouldn't have sat even if there were; she needed to get this said, and it seemed best spoken on her feet.

"Igraine, we've been over this. We have no choice in this matter. As the only heir of my bloodline, it falls on you to maintain the Veil that guards our people. I cannot do it for you. Only you can keep Dumnonia safe and that safety requires that you wed Uther and join our kingdom with his. I cannot release you from this, Daughter." Heavy and resigned, his words hung between them.

"What if I say no, Father? What if I refuse?" Igraine had never said this out loud, only tossing the words around in her head at night when she couldn't sleep.

He said nothing, glancing somewhere over her right shoulder, at a blank spot on the wall. Igraine almost thought his hearing was failing him as well when at last, he spoke.

"Then your people die, Igraine. Everyone dies, and it will be your fault."

It was her turn for silence. *How could he put all this on me, her mind screamed. She wasn't the king, and yet the safety of everyone in the kingdom was now her burden to bear? It was beyond cruel.*

"I cannot believe that, Father. Surely, the gods would not abandon us whether the Veil exists or not. We lived for centuries without it. Your father and his fathers before him needed no Veil, no sorcerer to hold their lands safe. What does that say about you?" Igraine heard the echo of cruelty in her own words, but she didn't care. *What kind of king allows his daughter to pay the price for his people?*

"Go. There is nothing more to say between us now. Do what you will, but you know the price." He stood from his seat and turned his back on her, heading toward his privy chamber, slamming the great oak door behind him. The sound shuddered through her, muffling the sound of footsteps from the outer hall.

"Don't let him scare you, Igraine. He's all bluff and bother; he's been like that since he was a child. If anyone dared challenge him, he'd pitch such a fit until he had his way. Nothing much has changed." Ithyl said from behind her, causing her to jump as if she were Longshanks. She spun on her heel to face the burly man.

"By Ceridwen's cauldron, you scared me to death, Uncle. I did not hear you." Igraine's hand had reached out for the edge of the table to steady herself. Until recently, her uncle had always been away from Tintagel, patrolling the frontier. They'd hardly spoken more than a dozen times over the years.

"Apologies, I've never been said to have a light footfall. Certainly, no lighter now that I am here, idle, and happily wed. Does make me yearn for time on my horse, patrolling with my men. Although, what kind of man wishes away peace for war, eh?" He crossed over to the papers Geraint had been studying and lifted them toward the candlelight.

"I should be going. I've upset Father and myself in the process. I hope you will find him in better spirits. Good evening, Uncle."

"Err, yes, good evening, Igraine. And remember, he's not the one that has to marry Uther. Do what your heart tells you, eh?"

♛

IGRAINE MADE her way from her father's rooms toward her quarters, aware of the late hour from the dark halls and quiet rooms. The castle was never truly at rest - someone was always about tending to fires or cleaning or on guard. Still, in this dark moment, there were hardly more than the young woman and the mice to be heard in the hallways. *Longshanks must be slacking at his job.*

To get to her chamber from the king's rooms, Igraine had to enter the Great Hall and cross toward another part of the castle. Unlike earlier, it was dimly lit. There were only one or two people scurrying about, cleaning up from those who had recently left for bed. Igraine spied a tall form still bent over his wine, and she recognized his blond hair. Uther.

"Lady Igraine, you've recovered, I see." He chuckled and raised his cup in salute. Igraine turned to walk toward his table.

"Yes, it was miraculous. All better now. I see you are more like a bat and not a dove; does something keep you awake tonight?" It was an impertinent question, perhaps, but she suspected he wouldn't mind talking about himself.

"I prefer the wee hours, I always have. I sent my retinue on without me so I could gaze into my wine and ponder my future in silence. Little did I know that my own bride would be coming to join me. Please, sit." He gestured toward the bench, and Igraine took a spot opposite him. He offered her a cup, but she shook my head; she had definitely had enough to drink. His hand looked soft and smooth in the dim light of the nearby fire.

"I am afraid that I am not much company right now. I've upset my father, and I suspect that will be a sin I will be paying for tomorrow...err...today, I suppose, since dawn isn't too far away." He peered at her over his cup, eyes quizzical under his furrowed brows.

"How have you upset him if I may ask?"

She took a moment to decide whether to lie or tell the truth.

"I told him I did not wish to marry." *He might as well know where her heart was in all of this.*

"I see," he said, without any sound of anger or even concern. They could have been discussing a crop of barley or the price of tin for trade.

"I am sure this doesn't surprise you, My Lord. After all, we do not know each other. I am not a woman who wishes to wed a stranger, duty, or no. I am sorry."

"I understand completely, My Lady. I have held the same thoughts throughout the entire ride here. You are not the only one not keen to wed a stranger. No offense meant, of course." He set down his cup and took the bold step of taking her hand in his. It was just as soft as it looked.

"Igraine, I have made peace with my future. It is not as I would have wished it, but my duty comes before all else. We are the same in that. I cannot promise that you will come to love me, but I can promise I will never give you cause to hate me. I will treat you with honor. You will someday be queen of my kingdom, and together our child will rule our two countries as one. Is that not enough for a life?" With a squeeze, he let her hand go and stood up, looking like a younger version of her own father in his gaze.

"I don't know, Uther. The life I thought was mine is now not my own," Igraine said, gazing up at the handsome stranger who was supposed to share her bed. "Can a life really be yours if you have no say in how it unfolds?" She felt the tears at the corner of her eyes, and she blinked them away.

"No one's life is truly their own, Igraine. Not a peasant and not a king. You're learning now that you, too, must make the best of what is before you. Good night, My Lady." Uther left her sitting at the table, wondering if she was being a love-sick fool.

CHAPTER ELEVEN

1984

"What do you mean, 'I'll take him'?" Arty said to the little girl who was munching happily on her scone.

"Back. I'll take you back. To the past, of course." Lowen responded as if he were the dumbest person she had ever met. *Maybe he was, he thought.*

"You mean time travel? Alright, so how does that work exactly?" His hand was back on the doorknob. This conversation just got even crazier.

"Arty, you wanted proof, and that's what we'll give you. Lowen will take you back in time, not back to Igraine yet - we aren't prepared for that. Just something small and easy. Say, one hundred years into the past, right here at Tintagel?" Morgan said, directing the question to her daughter. The orange-haired girl nodded sagely.

"That didn't answer my question. How does it work?" Morgan was already rising from the table and heading over to a shelf of jars. If they expected him to take some kind of potion, that wasn't going to happen. *No hallucinogenic mushrooms for me, thank you very much, he thought.*

"Explaining how time travel works is like explaining how birds fly to a fish. What I can tell you is that by combining my magic and certain plants, we can create a doorway, a path back in time. Since you do not possess the ability to travel in time on your own, Lowen has to come with you as a guide. Lowen, unlike myself, is impervious to the major side effect of time travel it seems. For this reason, she'll go with you."

"What side effect?" Arty asked as the kid finished her scone and bolted over to her mother's side to grab some jars.

"Age. It makes you older." Lowen said, opening the lid of a glass jar and holding it up to her mother's nose. Morgan shook her head violently.

"That's gone rancid, Lowen. Toss it out."

"Excuse me, so if I go back in time, it will make me older? How does that work?"

Both of them exchanged a look that could only be exasperation. "Movement through time has a price. For most people, it adds age to your physical body - maybe only a year or two, depending on the travel. Lowen is lucky because it doesn't do that to her. Then again, her father was full-blooded *sidhe* and High Born, so that would explain it." Morgan replied as if that answered any question he might have. *Far from it.*

"So, I will lose a year of my life if I go on this little hop back a hundred years with Lowen? Why the hell would I do that? Sorry, this isn't what I signed up for when I came to Tintagel." Arty opened the doorknob and stepped out into the sunlight, already feeling better among the peonies and foxgloves.

"Wait! You have to go back. Don't be scared." Lowen called from inside the house as he stepped off the small porch. Her tiny feet pounded on the floor as she ran out to him.

"Arty, look, we aren't supposed to tell you your future, it isn't a good idea to know what happens to you, but you have to go back because if you don't...well..." She paused, glancing at her daughter, who now stood near the doorway.

"If you don't, your whole family line will cease to exist. You need to go back to save yourself."

Morgan's words buzzed around him in the sunlight, but he couldn't quite understand them. *To save himself?* But he existed, his family existed. *If something happened in the past to end his family line, would he be standing there?*

"Look, when the past was new, I was the one who stopped Igraine. You like record albums, don't you, Arty?" Morgan said, startling him. *What did albums have to do with this, he wondered.*

"Alright, picture an album on a turntable, spinning, and spinning. The first time you play it through, everything is smooth, no scratches. The first song on the album still spins even as the needle plays the album's last song. Now, imagine that something happens to that album, and the first song gets a scratch on the vinyl. It is never going to play the same again. That is what has happened here. There is a scratch that has prevented me from stopping Igraine in the past. If that scratch isn't fixed, the song ends."

He thought he understood what she was saying with her strange metaphor. Something had scratched time, and they needed him to fix it. *Or at least, that is what he thought they were saying.*

"Alright, but you still have to prove to me this whole thing is real. If it is, I will help you. If it isn't, I am calling the police. Do we have a deal?" Morgan nodded, and Lowen ran back inside.

HE FOLLOWED BEHIND THE PAIR, walking toward the ruins of the castle. His lunch break from orientation was almost over, but Lowen laughed when he pointed that out.

"It doesn't work like that, Arty. You won't be late. We could stay back in time for a year, and it wouldn't seem we were gone even a minute. You'll see."

The ruins had visitors, and they wove their way between couples taking photos of each other against the picturesque horizon. Morgan led them toward an archway; the only thing that remained of some ancient wall. Arty could just make out some stone-carved stairs on the other side, leading down a hill.

"We're here. This is the doorway that will take you back. We need to anoint the stones, and then when I am ready, Lowen will lead you through. You'll want to take off your watch, though. It won't survive the journey, I'm afraid." Morgan pointed to his Timex, the one his father had given him when he graduated high school.

Arty unlatched the watchband while watching Morgan dab the stones with her fingertips, wet from the contents of a glass jar in her hands. She was murmuring something, but her voice was too low to hear, and he imagined the words were ones he wouldn't know anyway. Lowen reached out and took his hand in hers. They stood like this for several minutes, before Morgan stepped aside.

"There and back, Lowen. No detours, no sightseeing. Every trip has its risks, so be careful and hurry back."

"Yes, Mum," the little girl said as she pulled him toward the doorway. His feet were lead. He was either going back in time, or he would be the biggest fool - and he didn't want either.

"Are you sure we can get back," Arty asked as the girl pulled him over the threshold. Whatever answer Morgan was going to give was lost in the sound of howling wind.

They were soaked, almost immediately. Dark storm clouds ravaged the skies, and every inch around them had rivulets of water. Arty almost slipped on the stone step as Lowen pulled him through the arch. It was daylight, but just barely, and it was freezing cold.

"Good Lord, are we here? Where are we?" The girl released his hand and scampered down the stairs, oblivious to the rain soaking her jumper. Her orange hair was a wet mat on her head.

"Follow me, Arty. Hurry," she called, following the bend of the stairs, out of his sight. He couldn't recall feeling such terror before with the loss of his pint-sized guide.

"Wait! Lowen, don't go!" He yelled above the roaring wind, grabbing onto the nearby rock edge as he tried to hurry after her. He could have been the only human for all he could see in the gray rain.

Arty turned the corner, and there stood two men, each clad in what looked like black slickers but much thicker and heavy looking. They had boots on their feet that didn't look like any galoshes he had ever seen. Both had hoods on, and one of them held a cane. Lowen was nowhere to be seen.

He realized he was standing before them wearing jeans and a striped blue sweater, no coat or hat, and drenched to the bone. Luckily, their hoods had blocked out the sound of his approach; they had yet to see him.

"Duck," Lowen whispered, from behind a large stone to his right. Arty felt her hand tugging on his pant leg. He squatted quickly and shuffled behind the rock. From the cleft in the rock, he saw one of the men turn to look our way.

"Did you hear something, Mortimer?" One man tapped the other one on his shoulder. The man with the cane turned to look toward him.

"I can't hear a thing, Baines, not above this racket. This was a wasted trip, damn weather is too awful to actually enjoy the site. We should head back to the village. I need some whiskey to warm up with and a fire. Any more of a chill and I'll warrant we will both come down with a case of the ague. Let's be off." The man turned, heading back down the hillside, leaning on his cane. The other man continued to stare toward the rock that was shielding the pair from view.

"I could have sworn I heard a child's voice. Strange. Must be some pixies playing tricks, eh?" He chuckled and followed his companion down the slick steps, taking care not to take a tumble. When both men were well away from us, Lowen stood up.

"See? I told you the truth. Believe me now?" She darted her tongue out at Arty and started walking back toward the arch. "Come on, Mum will be worried. Let's go." He trailed behind her back toward the top of the hill.

♛

ARTY'S CLOTHES were still wet as he stepped into the sunshine, feeling that roar of wind slamming against his ears as Lowen pulled him along. Waiting for them was Morgan, holding his watch.

"Oh, dear, you're all wet. Sorry about that. Odds are good that the weather might not cooperate, but I had hoped you wouldn't get drenched. You can tell Dr. O'Malley that you slipped in a puddle on your walk." She handed Arty his watch and turned to head back down the hill. Lowen had scampered ahead to hold her hand.

"Everything alright, my girl?" Morgan asked, and the child nodded. "Good."

"And that's it? Just like that?" Arty asked, hurrying to catch up with them.

"Yes, that's it. I take it you're convinced now? The rain alone should have done that. You weren't seen, were you?"

"No, Mum. We weren't seen. Two old men were nearby, but you know me, quick to find a good hiding spot."

"Well done, Lowen. And now, Arty, I believe we have your word that you would help us?"

He was convinced that something had happened, but just what that was, he couldn't say.

"I did say that," he sighed as he felt the water squelching in his shoes. "I guess I'm on the hook."

CHAPTER TWELVE

Igraine had barely closed her eyes when they flashed open from Gisela's calling. Dawn streamed through the windows, and she rubbed at her crusted lashes. *Why in the world is she rousing me so early?*

"Lady Igraine, your father bids you rise for riding. You must hurry to him, they leave at once." Gisela held a pair of woolen stockings for the sleepy woman to put on.

"Where are we going? What has happened?" Igraine asked, letting Gisela pull her from the bed and tug the nightdress over her head.

"There's been a breach in the Veil. The Saxons are raiding."

THE RIDERS WERE ASSEMBLING in the stables, with pages scurrying to get the horses saddled quickly. The king was there, though not dressed for riding. Ithyl, Uther, Morgan, and Merlin were already astride their horses as Igraine joined the rest of the guards hurrying to their saddles.

"Your father wishes you to ride with us, Lady. To see just how vital the Veil is to our protection and what happens if there is a breach. He stays behind to see to other matters," Merlin said, giving Geraint a short nod. *No doubt, he stayed behind because of his eyesight, but none would say so, Igraine thought.*

"Can you ride, Lady?" Uther asked, and it wasn't so foolish a question as it might have seemed. A princess might be expected to embroider or dance, but she wasn't always expected to ride well.

"Yes, I've ridden across these cliffs and as far as the tin mines. I'll manage, thank you." He smiled and gave her horse a pat. Something about that gesture set her teeth on edge. *Perhaps I just haven't slept enough to keep a good humor.*

"Then what are we waiting for? Let's be off." Ithyl gave his horse a light kick to the sides, and he took off from the stables, heading toward the landbridge, with his men behind him. The riders streamed after him in the pinkish light, riding toward the sunrise.

It may have been near the summer solstice, but it was still chilly, and Igraine was grateful for her woolen stockings as her legs clamped the sides of Shadow, her horse. Morgan was behind her, managing her horse with little trouble, and Uther rode at the front with Ithyl. Merlin brought up the rear in the train as they crossed the landbridge toward the mainland. *The Gloria* bobbed in the harbor below. Igraine wondered if Arthur slept in his bunk.

Reaching the firm cliffside, she gave a slight breath of thanks. Shadow was sure-footed, but heights were something that she had feared as a child. It was nice to be on broad land where a tumble from her saddle wouldn't send her crashing into the sea.

"Igraine, may I ride with you?" Morgan asked, bringing her horse parallel. They were riding at a brisk pace to keep up with Ithyl, but Morgan held her horse steady.

"Of course. Do we know what has happened with the Veil? How were they able to breach it?" Steam puffed with Igraine's words as they rode.

"That I cannot say. Nothing should have been able to breach it. The sigils are still in place, the magic should be strong. Unless the Saxons have a sorcerer of their own to help pierce the Veil, I don't see how it could be done." Morgan wondered if any sorcerer had the power to overcome something constructed by the venerable Merlin.

"Do we know how many have entered Dumnonia? Where are they gathered?" Igraine had never been further from Tintagel than the tin mines, so anywhere else on the map could have been as far away as Rome for all she knew.

"They have invaded near the farming round of Gavelford. Father says there are maybe twenty or thirty of them, a large scouting party. They must not be allowed to advance, and we cannot let them leave with the knowledge of the kingdom." Morgan's words were growing fainter as her horse drew back slightly. The terrain was rough, and they wouldn't be able to ride abreast for much longer.

"What is the answer, then?" Igraine asked, imagining a band of Saxon barbarians waiting for them in the oat fields.

"We must defeat them, Lady," she said before falling back.

♛

THE MORNING SUN crawled along the sky, but they didn't stop to rest the horses or take a drink for themselves. A faint smoky haze clung along the horizon that they rode toward, and Igraine thought it was only morning fog rising in the crisp air. The closer they came to it, the harder it was to believe that. Something had been set on fire.

Visibility was good as they traveled the cart path toward Gavelford; there were no glens or thickets to hide warriors who might ambush the party. Uther had silently signaled his men with hand gestures, and they had fanned out on either side. Their horses stomped through the newly sprouted fields of oat. The farmers of Gavelford wouldn't thank them for that, Igraine felt certain. As they crested the small rise that led into the town, it hit her that the farmers had much bigger things to worry about. The town was a smoldering pile of cinders.

"By the Goddess, what has happened here," Igraine asked though she knew her own answer. Someone had set the town's round buildings on fire, burning through the straw roofs and woven fences, the animal shelters, and the merchant stalls. It was nothing but charred rubble.

"Lady, you should stay back, we don't know if it is safe," Uther called over his shoulder, gesturing for her to halt.

"No, the Lady must see. Whatever the cost paid here, she must see it." Merlin's voice replied from behind. He drew his horse alongside Igraine and gave her a long look before giving his mare a light tap in her flank with his spur.

The air had a strange smell, a mix of fire with something else, something Igraine didn't want to think about. *Where had the people in this village gone? Were they among the blackened bits piled on either side of her, Igraine wondered.* She held the edge of her sleeve to her face to filter the air; her sleeve smelled of lavender and the kitchens back in Tintagel. Homey and comforting in this scene of chaos.

"There, someone is moving, over there," Ithyl shouted, and his troop of warriors followed him. The horses followed the procession to a small building, only missing its roof. Sitting on the ground was an old man, leaning against the wattle and daub walls.

"You are too late," the man muttered as Ithyl climbed off his horse and approached him.

"What happened here? Tell us."

"They came. The invaders came. We couldn't stop them, we had no shields, no pikes, nothing but some axes and spades." The old man stared ahead at the horse's feet as if he didn't even see Ithyl standing there. Ithyl squatted to the man's level to gaze in his eyes.

"Grandfather, who attacked you? Did you see any colors or badges? Help us find them."

"A golden monster, on a field of red. One rider carried a banner. That's all I saw before…" He stopped, letting large tears drip from his ash-rimmed eyes. They streaked down his wrinkles, traveling down the ropey edges of his neck.

"Wessex," Uther said to no one in particular. Dumnonia's neighbors to the east had breached their lands, through Merlin's impregnable Veil.

"Did none other survive?" Ithyl asked, patting the old man's arm before standing up straight.

"We none survived. They came, they took no one. No one was captured, just pushed us into the buildings and set them alight. Why would they do that?" Finally, the old man raised his head, not to look at Ithyl, but to raise his question to the skies. If he heard an answer, he didn't say.

"Search for survivors," Ithyl said, his voice flat with doubt. With a final pat on the old man's shoulder, he turned back toward his party, drawing close to Merlin.

"Sorcerer, how did they breach your defenses? Surely, the Veil should have prevented this attack."

Merlin shifted slightly in his saddle; whether it was from discomfort in the seat or the question, Igraine could not be sure. "I will need to seek that answer, My Lord. As I have said before, I was able to draw the Veil across the land, but it is not within my power to hold it there - that falls to another. The Veil is weakening, as I warned you." He didn't look at her, but Igraine knew exactly what he was saying.

"But, if the Veil can be breached, then Geraint may be wrong to place his faith in magic to defend his kingdom. The soldiers of Dumnonia kept these lands safe, even when the Romans invaded. We needed no magic then, and perhaps, we need no magic now. A strong sword arm is always the best defense." Ithyl climbed back into his saddle and gave a nod to his man-at-arms nearby. A group of soldiers rode away from the village, looking for the Wessex marauders. Igraine had no faith they would find them.

"Ithyl longs for the days of his youth, when he patrolled the borders and when men put their faith in his might. He forgets that it is a different time. The Romans held Wessex and Mercia at bay. That defense is gone." Merlin said, for Uther's benefit, as he watched the prince stare at the smoldering ruins. "Maintaining the Veil is how we protect this land, and your kingdom as well. It is good that the ceremony comes soon. I will seek answers to this breach in my chambers."

The sorcerer turned his mare back toward Tintagel, with Morgan following close behind. Ithyl and his men were still scouring the village, leaving Uther and Igraine at the center of the destruction.

"What say you, Lady?" Uther asked, turning slowly to look at his bride-to-be from under his helmet. He held the reins lightly in his soft hands.

"I do not know, My Lord. What we see here is a travesty, but I wonder how it could happen at all if the Veil is the salvation that the sorcerer claims. Yet, if the Veil were gone, would all of Dumnonia face this fate? I cannot say."

Uther nodded in thought, mulling her words over. They seemed to match his own mind. *If the Veil was the protection, what had happened here? Would the whole Veil fray and fall in the days ahead?*

"Igraine, I know your heart is not resolved to marry. I think we must think on this because the voices of these dead souls demand it of us. If our union would prevent such devastation, I, for one, would pledge my bond to you to keep our lands safe. You'll have to decide such for yourself."

Uther looked at Igraine for a few still moments before turning his horse back toward the castle. Igraine hadn't decided whether to follow in his wake or stay behind to help. She desperately wanted to leave the village and forget everything she had seen, but the thought of heading back to the Great Hall and her father and everything waiting there left a cold lump in her gut. She needed something warm, something comforting to her body and soul. Only one place held that; Edith's kitchen and a sunny patch with Longshanks.

With a nod to Uther, she turned her mare back toward the sea and followed him back to the castle.

CHAPTER THIRTEEN

"My Lady, you look as wind-swept as a sylph in a storm. Where have you been?" Edith ushered Igraine to a seat at the wooden table where she was chopping cabbage. In the corner behind Edith, Igraine saw the little pitcher of goat's milk the cook left out nightly for her helper, the hobgoblin, Tân. At night, while she slept, he cleaned the fire's ashes and stocked the woodpile for her - in return for her payment of milk.

"I see Tân still visits, that's good to hear. Hardly any hobgoblins left in the castle as far as I know." Igraine said, changing the subject. She didn't want to tell Edith about the village, the fire, the old man, the sickening smell of burned flesh.

"He's a dear and loyal to boot, so long as he receives his night milk. I haven't had a chance to clean the pitcher yet, what with all the soldiers needing a meal. Where is that scullery lad anyway? Cled, where are ye?" She shouted his name, and they heard a scurry of feet coming from the larder. The small boy appeared with jam stains on his lips.

"Up to sneaking some jam, are we? You are lucky that I like you, boy. See to Tân's pitcher, will ye? And fetch the teapot for Lady Igraine." She gave the cabbage leaves a dreadful chop, and Cled hurried about his tasks, no doubt fearful that he could become a cabbage himself if he wasn't careful.

"Edith, how did you decide to wed your husband?" In all the talks the pair had shared, Igraine had never asked about him. He had died when she was just a little girl; she scarcely remembered him, other than his mop of red hair and his muscular arms hoisting Arthur on his shoulders. He seemed kindly in her memory.

"Such a strange question, Lady. Amlodd and I were wed so long ago, it hardly can be remembered. We jumped the broom over twenty years on now." She put down the knife and took a seat on the stool nearby, resting her large frame on the spindly legs.

"Amlodd was a horse groom for your grandfather, King Erbin, who built Tintagel. When I was a younger lass, I had my eye on a handsome falconer, whose name was....", she paused, chewing on her lower lip and gazing upward toward the low wooden ceiling. "That's odd, I can't remember his name to save my life, but he was a handsome thing, I recall that. All the lasses had their eye on him, but he paid us no mind. Still, Amlodd didn't let that stop him. He came right up to me one day and said, 'Edith, you and I will be wed.' And sure enough, we were." She chuckled and took the teapot from Cled. The boy handed Igraine an empty mug before hurrying back to the hearth.

"And you knew he was the one to marry? Was there a doubt in your mind at all?" Edith swirled the pot in her hands three times toward her right before she poured the hot tea into Igraine's cup. The scent of chamomile and lavender washed over them like a warm shawl.

"Doubt? What was there to doubt? He loved me. It was plain in his eye. And I loved him, bless his spirit. We'd have been fools to ignore that." Edith poured her own mug and watched her guest for a moment, clearly wondering about her questions. It was beyond peculiar for the Lady of the castle to be asking the cook about her love. Even as close and friendly as they were.

"I suppose it must have been easier for you, with no one to tell you what you must do. You could follow your heart, whatever it said."

"Lady, it is true that we weren't noble folk, and no princes were waiting in line for my hand. But princess or mere cook, the voice of the heart is the same, and it should be listened to." Edith smiled kindly, and Igraine knew she saw right through her. They both knew she was thinking of Uther and of Edith's son, Arthur.

"Thank you, Edith. The tea is very warming, as were your words. You've always been someone I could trust to speak truth to me. It means a great deal." Igraine said, rising from the little stool, still clasping the warm mug in her hands. Edith had work to do, and Igraine had a decision to make.

"Lady, I cannot claim to have known your mother, Enid, but I would wager to say that she would be proud of the woman you have become. Whatever you decide, I know it will be the right decision. May the Goddess help you find peace with it all."

Igraine smiled and headed toward the kitchen garden behind them, where she was sure she would find Longshanks hunting butterflies in the warming sunlight. She gave herself until the evening meal to decide her fate.

CHAPTER FOURTEEN

"Father, how was the Veil breached?" Morgan asked Merlin as she entered his chamber. He was leafing through a book and jotting notes on a small piece of parchment.

"Morgan, what makes you say the Veil was breached?" Merlin muttered, keeping his eyes on his list as she approached the table. She could just make out the words 'Comfrey' and 'Bloodroot.' *What kind of a potion was he making, she wondered.*

"Father, the dead villagers can answer that question. Is that not how they were killed, from a breach in the Veil?." Morgan stared at him, disbelief obvious on her face. *Was he losing his mind? We had just come from the scene of the massacre.*

"Daughter, what I tell others, and what I tell you can be two different things. The Veil is intact, weaker perhaps, but intact. My magic is as strong as ever. The villagers….were a means to an end." He put down his quill and looked up at his daughter, a stern look on his face.

"What do you mean? I do not understand." With a curious look, he stared at her as if he were examining her for faults, pursing his lips in consideration.

"I would have thought you would have known from the subtle

energy in the village, but perhaps your magic is not as strong as I thought. Let me explain, Morgan. There are times when we must do things that are for the greater good, whether we wish to or not. It is imperative that Igraine joins with Uther, that she produces a child. In order to secure this future, to convince the willful girl to do her duty, I made a slice within the veil to allow the marauders entry. I mourn for those lost, but it was necessary." He picked up his quill again, prepared to continue with his notes.

"You mean to say that you had those people murdered so Igraine would be sure to wed Uther? How could you do such a thing? Surely, the Morrigan will not look kindly on this act. Do you not fear the wrath of the gods for this?" She had never spoken to her father like that, never questioned his decisions in such a brazen way. His word was a law not to be broken, but the dead in that village gave Morgan courage.

"Do not question what you cannot understand. As I said, I did not wish to harm those people, but Igraine is willful, and I must ensure she unites with Uther. Whatever the cost."

"I hope it was worth it, Father. Even the fear of more invaders may not be enough to force Igraine's hand in this. This could have all been for nothing." Morgan said, longing for the sunny breezes outside the walls of Merlin's chamber. She needed to be away from the place, with its fetid air and dark corners. As his daughter and apprentice, his deeds spilled onto her, and she wanted them washed off.

"If the reality of death is not enough to force our princess to make the right decision, I will make her see reason in another way. As I said, Morgan, I will do what is necessary." His quill was scratching along the parchment as Morgan stepped out of his chamber and took a deep breath.

♛

THE EVENING MEAL was set in the Great Hall, platters arranged for all the soldiers and courtiers to stuff their bellies. The crew of *The Gloria* was there too; a farewell meal before they weighed anchor tomorrow. The room was full and full of fear.

"My Lady, Morgan, have you seen Lady Igraine?" Uther asked Morgan as he scanned the room, looking for his betrothed. She shook her head in reply.

"No, Prince Uther, I have not. She has not appeared all day, but I am sure she is safe. This morning's visit to the village was upsetting to us all." The sorceress took her seat at the High Table, near Uther, with her father at the far end by King Geraint. If Igraine was even half as upset as she was, Morgan feared she wouldn't come to the meal at all. She only came because of Merlin's wrath if she did not.

"I understand, of course, but being alone won't ease her mind. She needs to find her peace with her friends and those who care for her." Uther raised his goblet, taking a sip of his ale. His bride-to-be was more naive than he would have guessed when he agreed to marry her two years ago. Naive, but she had a good heart. Knowledge and patience would come with age, he was sure.

"She has many friends within the castle; I am sure she is doing just that," Morgan replied, gazing across the tables of chattering people, all talking about the village burning. Ithyl and his men had found no survivors. The old man had died on his way back to the castle with them.

They saw the door open across the room, and Igraine stepped in, dressed in a somber, dark red dress. Seeing her made Morgan realize just how much she had hoped the young woman would stay away, now that Morgan knew about Merlin's terrible trick. It was as if Morgan had been a party to his deed, and seeing Igraine's sad face drew a wave of guilt crashing on her. *How can I face her, knowing what he has done, Morgan wondered.*

"Ah, there she is," Uther said, and he raised his goblet toward her in a gesture of hello. She wove her way between the tables as a shuttle through a loom, eventually reaching the High Table.

"Good evening, Uther, Morgan. I am sorry that I was late. I lost track of the day." Igraine said, taking her place next to Morgan. Both the king and Merlin acknowledged her with a nod.

"Are you well, Lady? I was worried perhaps today had distressed you." Uther said.

"I do not know how anyone can be well on a day such as today, but I am not ill, My Lord. Thank you for asking. I have been lost in thought, but my mind is much clearer now." She glanced slightly to her left, to the table where the crew of *The Gloria* dined and where Arthur's tall frame sat a good foot above the others. The two exchanged a glance and a smile.

"I am glad to hear you are better, Igraine. I never wish you to be distressed," Uther replied simply before receiving a plate of fish from the page who served him. The king called to him and drew him toward their conversation, leaving Igraine and Morgan alone to speak.

"Lady," Morgan said, not sure what she would tell her, but fearing she would be sharing Merlin's secret if she spoke another word. Lies did not stay lightly on her lips.

"Morgan, it is alright. Everyone has been trying to convince me what I should do. My father, your father, Uther, my uncle. Everyone knows what is best for my life and my happiness and the safety of the kingdom. Now, at last, I know my own mind and what is best for me. I do not need anyone to make it up for me. After the meal, I will tell my father." Her words were crisp, with no hesitation in her voice. Her eyes had no tears, no clouds of doubt. Whatever she had decided, there would be no changing her mind.

"And would you tell me what you have decided?" It was bold to ask. Morgan held no standing beyond a tutor for this princess; despite Morgan's hopes, they were not yet close enough to be considered friends. And yet, she asked.

"I will not marry Uther. Despite the risk to the Veil, I cannot commit myself to a lifetime with a man I do not love. There must be another way to protect the kingdom. That is for your father and my father to discover. As much as I want to protect the people, this is more than I can do."

The guilt that had been lapping at Morgan's insides pulled back, a receding tide that left her feeling calm for the first time in hours. Merlin's deadly trick had not worked on Igraine, and Morgan was glad.

"I wish you well, Lady Igraine. And I admire your courage to stand for your heart and its desires. You honor me by telling me this. Thank you."

For the first time, Igraine looked at Morgan as if the sorceress had surprised her. In all the years they had known each other, in all the days spent in lessons and scoldings and lectures, she had never looked as astonished as she did right then.

"You aren't angry with me, Morgan? I was sure you would be, as will be Merlin and my father. And Uther, I suppose."

"No, Lady. I am not angry. I am proud of you."

A tear appeared in Igraine's eye, clinging to her lower lashes. When she smiled, it tipped over and scurried down her cheek.

"Now, I must face the wrath of men who always know best, Morgan. Do you have a potion for more courage you can make quickly?" She laughed, and though Morgan knew she was still afraid to tell them, she also knew nothing would stop Igraine.

CHAPTER FIFTEEN

"I need to speak with you, Father," Igraine said, waiting until the meal was over, and she could approach the king with a whisper in his ear.

"Igraine, what is it?" he said, loudly enough for Merlin to turn to look at them. Uther and Morgan were in conversation or at least had the grace to appear so.

"May we adjourn to your private rooms? I would rather not speak here in the Hall." She wasn't sure he would agree with the suggestion, but instead of dismissing it, he stood up.

"Bring wine to my chamber," he told the nearest page, before pushing back his chair and turning toward the door leading to his privy chamber. Merlin, uninvited, rose as well.

"I suspect this matters to me as well, Lady," he said, by way of explanation, before following Geraint toward the hallway. *Foolish to think I could speak about my life with my own father unaccompanied by his sorcerer.*

The king's rooms were cold; his servants had let the fire wane, not expecting him back until it was time to retire. They scurried to bank up the flame as he tossed his cloak on a chair for them to hang up.

"Does this have to do with the attack by the Saxons," he asked, not waiting for them to leave the room. The last thing Igraine wanted was to feed court gossip with eavesdropping.

"Yes, and no," she replied, waiting for him to settle himself near the hearth. Even though it was chilly, she stood away from the pair of old men sitting with their wine goblets.

"It only demonstrates the need…" Merlin began, but she cut him off with a raised hand.

"Please, Lord Merlin, let me say what I must say. I have considered everything most carefully, including the safety of the people, and my own heart. I know you wish for me to fulfill this prophecy, to keep the Veil intact for our kingdom and for Uther's, but Father, I cannot do it. As Uncle Ithyl says, my grandfather needed no such Veil to guard us. What you ask is too much. I will not wed Uther." The words sounded loud in the cold room, and Igraine heard the shuffle of feet somewhere behind her. In short order, the word would spread through the turris as a fire through a hayfield.

"Ithyl should mind his own business. He is not king. I am, and I have commanded it." Her father's jaw was set, teeth clenched, and his milky eyes narrowed.

"Father, I would rather not break your command, but I will do so if you do not release me from this arrangement. Whatever the consequences. I cannot do what you ask of me. I would regret it for the rest of my life."

"Merlin, speak sense to this girl, she won't listen to me."

The sorcerer sipped at his wine, his gold and ruby rings flashing in the firelight.

"My King, if the girl is not willing, we shall find another way. Let us discuss the safety of the kingdom and what lies ahead."

King Geraint opened his mouth to object to Merlin's words of release, but nothing came out. Igraine heard him take one breath and then another as if that would fuel what he could say in reply, but finally, he said simply "Go, Igraine. Let me talk to my sorcerer."

Without waiting for him to change his mind, Igraine bolted for the door. Around the corner, the feet were scurrying away, making sure she didn't catch their owners listening at the door. Her own feet were hardly on the stone floor; she couldn't believe that the old men had given up so easily. *Could it be true that I was released from my bond of marriage? I have to find Arthur to tell him what I have done.*

Back in the Great Hall, the crew of *The Gloria* was mostly gone - only Hereca and the captain remained, arguing over a game of dice where Hereca was clearly winning. Arthur was nowhere to be seen.

"Hereca, have you seen Arthur?" Igraine asked, interrupting the Hunnish pirate as she was giving the man a tongue lashing.

"He just left, if you hurry, you can catch him. Just as I caught this dog cheating." She gave the dice a throw, scattering them on the stone floor behind her.

"You're as daft as that pointy skull of yours, Hereca. I wasn't cheating!" Igraine hurried from the table before she could hear the reply, hoping to catch Arthur before he headed back to the ship.

Out in the night air, she smelled smoke - from the fires burning to warm the watchmen, no doubt - but it reminded her of the village. She shook her head, scattering both the scent and images from her mind. At the edge of the torchlight, Igraine saw Arthur's lanky frame about to turn from sight.

"Arthur! Wait, Arthur," she called, hurrying to catch up with him. He turned to look over his shoulder and stopped, his face brooding in the flickering light. She'd never seen him looking so solemn before.

"My Lady Igraine. I know I said I would stay but I have changed my mind. I must sail with the ship. Will you wish me farewell?" The firm set of his jaw reminded her of her father's.

"No, Arthur. I won't. I have good news," Igraine said, hoping her smile would bring about his own.

"Please tell me what you need to so I can be on my way."

His words stung, driving into her ears like an enemy's arrow. *What would make him so cold to me? Have I given him some offense beyond the pain of this marriage?*

"I am not going to wed Uther," she said simply, without the joy she had hoped to share just moments ago.

"You must."

It was all he said, staring at her in the torchlight. She watched the lock of red hair bob on his forehead as he nodded.

"Why would you say that? You know my heart, and I know yours." She raised a hand to touch his sleeve, but he bristled. *He doesn't want me to touch him.*

"I cannot be the reason that your people die. You have a duty, and I will not be the breach of it. I'm sorry, Igraine. I cannot." The words sounded like they were cutting his throat as he spoke them. His blue eyes were the color of wet stone, clouded, and dim.

"And just like everyone else, it is for you to tell me what to do, is it? First my father, then his sorcerer, then Uther, now you. All the men know what is best for me. I must remember to be so grateful that you can tell me what I ought to think and feel, Arthur. Truly." Igraine spat the words at him, rage twirling up her spine. Her hand, a second before ready to soothe, was now a clenched fist. *The gall of this man to tell me my duty, I cannot believe it.*

"Igraine," he said, his voice softer, but she stopped him just as she had stopped Merlin's speech before - with a raised hand.

"You cannot address me so. I am 'Lady' to you. You may feel you can tell me my path, but you cannot take away my standing. Good voyage to you and the crew, Arthur. I shall not trouble you again. But you should know, I am not going to marry Uther, whether you are here or not."

She didn't want to run from him, to appear weak and afraid to stand her ground. She wanted to walk regally back toward her rooms, head high and proud in the gloom of the night. But her body would not comply. Her feet started running, and with shoulders shaking, she wept, tears peeling down her face as the wind blew. He may have been shouting at her to come back, but all she could hear was her own sobs.

♛

"Lord Uther, thank you for joining us." Merlin swept his arm in a low bow, greeting the prince as graciously as he could muster. He wanted to be in Uther's good favor when he made this request.

"As you wish, Master Merlin. I am at your beck and call." Uther smiled at the old men, settling into a chair.

"We would not have bothered your rest, but the situation is quite dire," King Geraint said, glancing over to Merlin.

"Yes, quite dire indeed. I hope you understand that we have tried our best to resolve things before turning to this solution. This is not as we would have wished to proceed," Merlin said, picking up the narrative again.

"Gentlemen, please speak plainly. I have no idea what you are speaking about." Uther crossed one slim leg over the other and tapped his foot in the air.

"Igraine, as you no doubt have surmised, is a bit naive and headstrong. She doesn't understand how things work in the world, as she has always been sheltered and, I dare say, coddled. Forgive me, My King, for saying so." Merlin gave a quick glance to Geraint, but the king's expression did not change. He knew the truth of it.

"Yes, she is young, but she is smart and resourceful. I am sure she will grow into her duties with time." Uther's foot was almost fluttering, he was jiggling it so quickly. *Would these old men never get to the point, he thought.*

"Time is something we cannot wait for, I am afraid. As you know, we must have this union and defend both kingdoms. We have learned, just this night, that Igraine refuses to be joined...with you." Merlin's long fingers splayed as he spoke, gems flashing in the firelight. Uther's foot was still.

"I see. Well, if that is her decision, then what is there to say?"

The old men exchanged looks, and Geraint cleared his throat.

"Gentlemen?" Uther's eyes narrowed as he looked at their grave faces.

"I have a solution. It is not ideal, I warrant, but necessary. There is a way to have Igraine's compliance." Geraint stood up as Merlin finished his words, giving a slight bow of his head to Uther.

"Please excuse me," the king said. "I must retire."

Several moments passed before Merlin spoke again. "The king

does not wish to hear the particulars, despite approving of the basic idea. He understands what is at stake."

Uther's patience was gone, now that the king was no longer in their presence. "Speak plainly, Sorcerer. What is this plan?"

"You will seduce Igraine, and get her with child. The seduction shall be made easy by a potion that will transform you in her eyes to her own true love. Once it is done, she will come to her senses, and the Veil will be maintained." Those long fingers interwoven looked like a trap for a fox, catching prey with a quick snap.

"No," Uther said, standing and turning for the doorway.

"'No'? Is that all you have to say on the subject?" Merlin's fingers released and he used their strength to help rise from his chair.

"There is plenty I could say, Sorcerer. Words such as deceit, treachery, wicked, hateful, devious, and duplicitous. I could also say that I should run my sword through you for the mere suggestion of this. I could also say that any father who would do such a thing to his daughter is a tyrant and not worthy of joining with my kingdom. All these things I could say, but instead, I will merely say no. Do not ask me again. Ceredigion will protect itself and my party will depart tomorrow." Uther left the sorcerer clutching the table for support.

CHAPTER SIXTEEN

"Father, why have you summoned me?" Morgan entered the sorcerer's chamber. Merlin had a small copper pot suspended over his hearth, and he was bent over the flames.

"Morgan, you must take this brew and pour it into Uther's goblet in his chamber." He stood up stiffly, removing the pot with a wooden-handled poker, placing it gently on a stone slab on the table. The smell in the chamber was dreadful, something acrid and smoky with something sweet underneath.

"At this hour? He won't welcome such a disturbance, no doubt." She watched her father grasp the small handle of the pot in a fold of leather. He tipped the pot over a ceramic cup, and a thick greenish liquid streamed out.

"That is why you must be very sure he does not see you do this. It is vital that he drinks the potion without his knowledge. He cannot know, do you understand?" To Morgan's eyes, he seemed beside himself, wild-eyed and almost trembling. She couldn't imagine what had happened.

"Father, tell me what has you brewing potions in the middle of the night. Why must I do this, like a thief in the night? What is going on?"

He slammed the empty pot back onto the stone, sending small splatters of the noxious liquid onto his robes.

"Uther must lie with Igraine tonight. She must conceive a child for the prophecy, and the damn girl has broken off the marriage. She plans to leave Tintagel, as does he. We cannot wait for the solstice."

Now she knew why he looked desperate. Everything he had been planning hinged on Igraine's union with Uther, and now that was over.

"And this brew, it will do what to Uther? Force him to lie with her?" Morgan had studied many of her father's books but never seen a spell that could do that. Only an incubus or a succubus had that sort of power, or so she thought.

"It is just a small spell, a way to help Uther understand his duty. The potion will soften his resolve as well as Uther's visage. He will look as Igraine's love, that fool sailor. But the potion only works for a very short time, and you are wasting it talking to me. Go and take it to him. Now!"

Did the king know of this defilement? How could they do this to Igraine and to Uther? She took a step back from the table.

"No, I won't do it, Father. It is an abomination. I won't be a party to it. Take it yourself if you must, but I will be warning Igraine of your treachery." She took another step back, and she felt her feet freeze to the floor. Her father's lips were moving, but she couldn't hear the words.

"Foolish girl, why did I think I could trust you? You are no better than the love-crazed princess. But you won't get in my way, Morgan. You'll stay right there until I return. Then we shall decide what is best for you, Daughter." Morgan watched her father gather the cup as he shambled toward the door. He must have conjured the potion with his own blood, a recipe that foul would require some kind of sacrifice. It must be the reason why he limped - and why he needed Morgan to run this errand.

"You disappoint me, girl," he said as he closed the door behind him. "I'll find a servant girl to do my bidding." She couldn't move, she couldn't speak; her father's spell held her fast against her will.

THE SERVANT gently opened the door to the prince's chamber. It would be custom to knock, to wait for the prince's valet to call her to enter, but the sorcerer had been adamant that she must make no noise to disturb Lord Uther. Master Merlin had brewed a tonic for his headache, he said, but Uther was too proud to take it. To Mara's eyes, the prince looked like someone who would be too proud and haughty. *No wonder the sorcerer had used subterfuge to help heal the stubborn man, she thought.*

Peeking inside the doorway, she saw the prince was nowhere to be seen. Muffled noises were coming from the privy room, and she smiled at her luck. Taking care of the call of nature had the man out of sight. *How lucky could she be?*

Merlin had admonished her to pour the tonic into the prince's wine goblet, making sure every drop found the wine. The small cup's contents were inside his pewter cup with a quick pour, just as the prince swept into the room.

"What are you doing here?" Mara had managed to get the cup behind her back before he saw her. She saw the prince swathed in a silken blue robe.

"I came to see if you require any more wine or food, My Lord. I see you still have a full cup. Shall I bring you more?" She gave a deep bow before rising to find Uther's eyes on her bodice.

"No, I have enough, thank you. I shall be retiring soon. I have what I need." Uther smiled at her, a smile she had seen often enough on the stable boy's face. Lord or peasant, nothing was different when it came to that.

"I could take your cup and your platter after you finish your wine if that would please you." Mara smiled in return.

Uther walked toward Mara, placing a hand on the cup that rested on the table. *The cup that held his healing potion, she thought. He must drink it, Mara. Merlin commands it.*

"I can think of a few things that would please me. Perhaps you can help me with those as well," Uther said, raising the cup to his lips.

After a moment's pause, he finished the wine before wiping his lips with the back of his hand. He held the cup out toward Mara.

"I will return shortly, My Lord." Before he could protest, Mara took the cup and backed from the room, keeping the empty cup in the other hand that was behind her back.

CHAPTER SEVENTEEN

Gisela had gone to bed, after waiting up for Igraine to help her undress. She could have managed on her own, but Gisela had insisted, and now Igraine was alone in her room by the fire, wide awake. *How can I sleep when my future was torn apart by Arthur's words?*

"It doesn't matter," she said to the walls. "I'm leaving Tintagel, with him or without him." It was the only thing she was sure of; she was going to see the world. Maybe she'd become a pirate like Hereca, sail the Mediterranean sea and visit Carthage or Rome or Byzantium. Igraine didn't have the first clue about how to sail, but she could learn. Maybe she could travel to Aquitaine or Francia and teach others how to read Latin. She had no idea beyond leaving the only place she had known.

Igraine heard the soft knock on her door and briefly wondered if Gisela couldn't sleep. She might be looking for a late-night game of Nine Men's Morris. Igraine padded to the door, drawing the woolen wrap tightly around her shoulders. She pulled the door open and gasped to see Arthur standing at her threshold.

"What are you doing here? You can't be here," she stammered. *How had he passed by the dozen guards between here and his ship?*

"Igraine, I must speak with you. May I come in?" He asked, speaking so softly she could barely hear him. His voice sounded huskier.

"If anyone catches you here…" Igraine stopped, letting the words end in her mouth. Her reputation would be ruined, certainly, but she remembered that she wasn't going to be there. *What did she care what they thought?* He clearly didn't care about the risk to his own neck by being there.

"Come in," she whispered, opening the door a bit more to let him slide in. He wore a long blue robe, something one of the knights of the castle would wear. *He must have pinched it to slip in unnoticed, she thought.*

"What is it?" Igraine went back to her chair by the fire, but he caught her hand before she could sit.

"Igraine, we don't have much time. I must be with you."

"Here? Now?" He clutched her close to his tall frame. He seemed bigger to Igraine - less the lean spear that was his namesake and more the soldier. But then again, Igraine had only been this close to him once before, on the beach.

"Yes, let's not waste a moment." The words didn't sound like him.

"I don't know…" Igraine said though she knew she wanted to be with him. What she didn't know was whether it was right to be together within the walls of Tintagel. They should get away and begin their future away from her father's keep. Still, being in his arms felt so safe, she didn't want to leave them.

"Igraine," he whispered, kissing her neck, nuzzling his face against her hair. His hands felt so soft against her arms. She could imagine them caressing her, sending shivers down to her toes. He smelled like oiled leather and lavender, not the salty sea.

"Do you love me? Truly," Igraine asked, pushing herself back a little so she could look into his blue eyes. She saw none of the teasing that was always found there. Instead, his eyes were pleading, earnest with passion.

"Yes, I do," he said, whispering as he pulled back in for another kiss. "We are destined, Igraine. Believe me." With another kiss, Igraine put any doubt from her mind, and she let him lead her to her bed, damn the consequences.

"And now, Daughter, what is to be done with you?" Merlin said to Morgan as he hobbled back into his chamber. She hadn't moved from the spot where his spell held her.

"Although it is done, I don't want you causing Lady Igraine distress with any tales you might tell. Yet, you are my child, and I do not wish to harm you. I must keep you two apart, at least for the time being. Perhaps you will come to your senses when you see the safety I have bought for the kingdom."

Safety paid by another, Morgan thought, though her lips couldn't form the words. Her father no longer, this man would be called Merlin by her from now on. *What he had done was nothing less than an abomination, she thought.*

"Morgan, I shall free your body, though not your tongue just yet. We need to take you somewhere else, and I don't wish to call attention to us. You must promise to behave yourself. If you do not, I will have to take more drastic measures. Do you understand me, Daughter?" Morgan blinked in response. He wasn't freeing her tongue because he didn't want to risk a countercurse. He had succeeded because he had caught her off-guard; that would not happen again.

Merlin mumbled to himself, saying the words that let her limbs release from their rigor. She felt the blood flow back into her toes and fingertips — the icy prickles diminishing as his words left his lips.

"Some wine will warm you up. I know your limbs feel frozen. Take a sip before we leave, it will help." Morgan declined his fatherly advice and shook her head.

"Suit yourself. I'll see that your new arrangement has provisions, though it may take me a bit of time with this leg of mine." He gestured downward and reached for a cloak he had on a peg in the wall. "We'll fetch you a cape as well, Morgan. It is cold in the cave."

IGRAINE BLINKED IN the dawn light, glad for the covers pulled tightly to her chin. She was naked in the bed, and the room was chilly. Gisela had not been in to stoke the fire yet. With a start, she remembered that she wasn't alone. Gisela could not find Arthur in her chamber. Igraine turned over quickly to see that the bed was empty next to her.

"Arthur," she said in a quiet voice, sitting up. The room was still.

She was glad he had the good sense to be gone before the servants and courtiers were up and about, but he could have at least said goodbye. Waking up alone wasn't how she would have wished to end their first night together. *Besides, we have plans to make.*

She scurried from the bed to find her robe on the floor. Luckily, the fire hadn't gone entirely out; she could bring it back to life with some stirring and a small spell that Morgan had taught her years ago.

"Heart of fire, cinder, and ash, ember, and tinder, glow be cast. Spark and light, bring Brigid's blessing to this hearth." Wisps of smoke drew up the chimney, and the old oak log glowed a cheery orange.

"Guess all those lessons weren't a waste, though not as Merlin intended," Igraine said aloud, rubbing her hands fiercely together for warmth. She dearly hoped Gisela would have some hot tea with her when she came to dress her.

Arthur's ship was leaving, and Igraine was going to be on it. *This will be my last morning in Tintagel, she thought. What will I bring with me? When will I tell Gisela?* The questions swirled around her head. Before she let herself get carried away by all of it, she knew she had to at least speak with Arthur. Nothing was certain until that happened.

She couldn't wait for Gisela to come to assist her; she needed to dress and find him this morning, as soon as she could. She pulled a dark green gown from her chest of drawers and found a linen shift to keep the scratchy wool off her skin. Igraine didn't need the fanciful brooches or jewels in her box or her hair braided; she'd find him without all the trappings of being a princess. *He'll have to get used to that anyway, she thought.*

The knock on the door startled her; it was far heavier than Gisela's usual tap. Igraine pulled on the heavy door to find King Geraint standing there, looking ashen.

"Father, what is it?" *Why in the world was the King of Dumnonia knocking on her door when any servant could have summoned her?*

"Igraine, come with me now. Something terrible has happened. Uther is dead."

CHAPTER EIGHTEEN

Uther's chamber was near the king's rooms, which meant most courtiers didn't have access; the halls were empty except for the royal pair of Tintagel hurrying in silence. Igraine couldn't imagine what had happened and her father hadn't said. There would be time enough for answers when they were in Uther's chamber.

The door to the room was ajar, but Merlin's frame blocked any view from the corridor. He was standing in a crooked fashion as if he favored his leg, and his face was haggard and worn. As they approached, he stepped aside so they could pass.

"Sire, there is no need to distress Lady Igraine with this. Prince Uther's body is terribly disturbed." He looked at her with concern.

"My daughter is made of stern stuff, Merlin. This affects us all, she should be here." With that response, Geraint led the way past the sorcerer into the chamber.

The room smelled of iron, something metallic in the cold air. Uther's blankets were strewn about, and a long blue robe, inside out from being pulled off, lay on the floor near the bed. Then Igraine saw him, lying on his bed, flat on his back, crimson red flowering from his chest. He had been stabbed.

"Were there no guards near his room?" Geraint stepped closer to help his failing eyes see the death on the bed before them. Igraine turned away slightly to examine the red dragon painted on the shield leaning against the wall. It was the symbol of his home, of Ceredigion, their ally.

"Sire, none were patrolling the halls last night. We saw no need for guards for the prince; Tintagel is secure and safe," Merlin replied, though Igraine didn't know what he meant by "we." *She wondered if he had decided the question or was someone else involved, perhaps Uther himself?*

"Who found him?" Geraint stepped back and turned to face Merlin. His face was a mask of anger.

"His chamberlain, when he came to wake him for the morning. I was on my way to see you, My King, when the man bolted from the room, nearly knocking me down. He is waiting in my chamber, instructed to speak to no one. This must be handled carefully."

"Carefully? We're in a bloody mess, Merlin. How will we explain the murder of the Prince of Ceredigion under our very noses! He was sleeping a stone's throw away from my own chamber, and he was killed. I don't know that any amount of care is going to solve this problem."

"Sire, we will find the one who did this, of that I am sure. Our men are loyal, they would never have done such a thing; neither would Uther's men. It must be an outsider. We'll lock down the castle and find the one who killed him. You have my word." Merlin's words were strong, but they didn't sound quite so sure to Igraine's ears. For the first time, she detected a waver to the old sorcerer's voice. Someone had interfered in his grand plans.

"See to it, Sorcerer. Use all your skills and find the one who did this. Bad enough we have Wessex barking at our heels on the border, we don't want a war with Ceredigion to the north. Do not fail me," Geraint said, heading back toward the hallway to his chamber. Igraine turned to follow him, but Merlin touched her arm to hold her back.

"Lady, may I ask you a few questions before you go?" *Such a change from his normal commandeering tone, she thought.*

"Yes, of course," she replied. Igraine kept Uther's body behind her, so she didn't have to see the red gore. The sight of the red dragon on his battle shield wasn't comforting either.

"When was the last time you saw the prince?" Merlin leaned a bit on a wooden chair near the cold hearth. She gestured that he should sit, but he stayed standing.

"At the evening meal. I don't recall seeing him after. My chamber is too far from here for me to have heard anything." He nodded thoughtfully as she spoke as if he were recalling the evening for himself.

"Yes, of course. I am just trying to determine who may have seen Prince Uther in his final hours. Nothing strange or unusual happened last night?" He stared at her from under those fierce white eyebrows of his.

"No, nothing," she lied, immediately thinking of Arthur in her room. *That has nothing to do with Uther; there is no need to tell Merlin about that, she thought.*

"Thank you," he said, gesturing that she was free to leave. He sat on the edge of the chair as she turned toward the door.

"Lady," he said, as she crossed the threshold. "Stay near the castle today. Things are not safe beyond the walls."

"My Lord Merlin, things are not safe *within* the walls." She walked away from the crumpled sorcerer.

♛

SHE COULDN'T GO BACK to her chamber, not after seeing Uther's body, streaked with blood; the image wouldn't leave her mind. *Who could have done such a thing, and why?* No one within the castle had any cause to harm the prince; he was a guest of the king and under his protection. The only thing aided by Uther's death was dividing their two kingdoms, and none among them would wish that.

"Lady, have you heard the news?" Gisela found her in the hallway as she headed toward the Great Hall.

"What have you heard?" Merlin had kept the page who found Uther secured, and yet somehow, the castle still knew of the tragedy.

"The prince... he's been killed," she replied in the quietest voice. She looked worried. *We all should be worried, Igraine thought.*

"Gisela, tell no one of this. The king must have time to decide what is to be done." Gisela saw the tears on her lady's lashes, and she leaned in to give her a quick embrace.

"Oh, My Lady, I am so sorry for you. And your wedding was just days away." *She doesn't know that I had called it all off just last night.*

"Don't be sorry for me, Gisela. Things are much more serious for the kingdom now. There is no cause to weep on my account, truly." Igraine gave her another embrace before hurrying on down the hallway. There was no sense in telling her about breaking her pledge to wed him; it would only stir up rumors, and there would be enough of those as it was.

Igraine hurried through the Hall, avoiding the glances of Uther's men as they sat clumped together. If Gisela knew, no doubt they did as well. Her father would have to address them soon. She didn't envy his work. They would be howling for blood over the death of their prince and who could blame them.

"Where are you off to, Igraine?" Igraine heard Laria call to her from her seat by the fire. She was sipping a steaming mug of tea; Igraine could smell the dried chamomile. Laria's stomach must be bothering her.

"Oh, I wanted to say farewell to my friends on *The Gloria*. But how are you feeling, Laria? You look a little pale." It was a clumsy attempt to change the subject, but it worked.

"Queasy, as I am most mornings. The tea is a great help, but I am certain it shall pass soon. It is a small price to pay, after all." Laria smiled, giving her belly a pat.

"Are you...." Igraine stammered, not sure whether she should say it out loud. Laria was a superstitious woman, but she smiled broadly at the question.

"Yes, we are having a baby. Ithyl is so pleased." Igraine leaned in to give her a kiss at the news.

"My blessings on you and the babe. How wonderful to hear it." Laria nodded before taking another sip of her tea.

"A son, a royal son for the house of Dumnonia. He shall be born in midwinter. A little duke here in the castle." She beamed, and Igraine nodded in agreement, keeping her smile very bright for Laria's benefit. There was so much danger in birthing a child, both for her and the babe. Igraine would be sure to ask Morgan to cast her spells to help protect them both.

"Tell me whatever you need, Laria. I will be happy to help you." Igraine said, before bidding farewell and heading for the doors. The death of Uther and the news of the baby, all in the same morning. Her head was spinning.

Outside, as expected, she saw Ithyl's men, gathered in a show of force. The castle would be under fierce guard until Uther's murderer was caught. Her uncle was not among them, which seemed strange to her. They hovered about, watching the squires and pages hurry in their tasks, the farrier heading toward the stables, the maids emptying chamber pots. Life in the castle went on, even under such a tragedy.

Arthur would most likely be at his ship, preparing to set sail. Igraine was still hurt that he had slipped away without a word of goodbye, especially after the night they had shared. It seemed so cold of him, so unlike the kindly boy that she'd known all her life. Still, she wouldn't let her hurt keep her from seeing him, and she needed him to know that there was still much to discuss. *We have a whole future to plan for.*

Igraine pressed through the soldiers, snaking her way through the throng so she could turn toward the cliffside and the moored ship. Beyond her vision, she heard voices and noise, the sound of metal clanking and shouts. The men blocked her view, but together they all started moving toward the sound. With a rush of hope, Igraine wondered if they had caught the assassin. It would hopefully bring a swift end to the nightmare of Uther's death.

"Make way, we have him. Do not touch him. He must remain alive." Igraine heard Ithyl's voice rise above the din. The soldiers murmured and pushed back, making way for their commander who led the procession. Her uncle stood tall, dressed in leather armor, holding a sword in his hand. Igraine smiled to see him, relieved at his command of the situation. The smile froze on her lips as Arthur followed him, chained and shoved by one of Ithyl's lieutenants. His face was a bloody mess.

"Arthur," Igraine shouted, pushing her way toward the front of the pack. The men were startled by her shout.

"Lady Igraine, this does not concern you," Ithyl said, sheathing his sword and stepping forward to stop her. Arthur looked at her through his swollen eye, blood tinting his orange-red hair.

"What are you doing? Release him!" Igraine shouted, finally reaching the bulking form of her uncle. The guards kept Arthur well out of arm's reach.

"Igraine, do not make a fool of yourself. We will talk later. Compose yourself." Ithyl whispered through his gritted teeth, close to her ear.

"Take the prisoner to the cells. Keep watch on him," he shouted to his minion, who nodded and pushed Arthur along the path, away from her.

"What are you doing, Uncle?" She was not heeding his instructions. Igraine wanted answers now.

"Igraine, he killed Uther. He must be turned over to the King of Ceredigion, when we bring him Uther's body, as amends for this crime. It's the only way to save Dumnonia."

She heard the words, but they floated over her, not registering any meaning. The ground under her swayed, and she felt her knees start to bend. Her vision went black, and she felt Ithyl's grip on as she began to fall.

♛

I AM TRAPPED in a cave at the edge of the sea, and no one can rescue me, Morgan thought. Merlin, powerful sorcerer that he is, knew where to put me to keep me out of his way.

"Morgan, you'll be safe here. I'll ensure no harm comes to you, but I can't have you meddling right now. I need the plan with Igraine to go forward, and you might interfere. Reflect on your duty, Morgan; use this time to decide your future path. I do not want to cast you out, Daughter, but I will if I must. Have no illusions that your power is greater than my own."

Merlin's words still echoed in her mind, though he had been gone for hours. The cave was cold, but he had left her a brazier to warm the corner where a bed, a basket of food, and a stack of books were laid out. Within this corner, she sat behind a wall of crystal.

Merlin had sealed the corner with conjured crystal, knowing that any magic she might try could not penetrate it. Crystals amplify magic, but they can also confound it, and Merlin knew this as well as Morgan. He had put her in a box, and here she would stay until he was ready to let her out.

"At least he left me something to read," she muttered, pulling the tallow candle closer to the stack to inspect it. She was in the deepest part of the cave, away from the mouth that was fed by the sea. Somewhere above her, Tintagel was waking to a new day.

"How charitable," a voice replied, coming from the other side of the crystal wall. She could hear it, but she couldn't see the speaker through the milky barrier.

"Who is there?" Morgan rose from the pile of furs and straw matting on the floor. The light from the candle glinted off the crystal surface.

"Lady Morgan, I've long wished to make your acquaintance. I wish it were under better circumstances, but here we are." It sounded like a man speaking, but the voice had a lilt to it, a sound unknown to her.

"I say again, who is there?" This time she spoke softly, finding a part of the cave wall to press her back up to. She had no weapons, nothing beyond her own magic to protect her. She had to hope Merlin had spoken true about protecting her.

"There is no reason to be afraid. I would never hurt you. Your mother was one of my people; we are practically kin, Morgan. Fear not." A spot on the crystal, not far from her, began to glow as if someone lit a lantern within it. Prisms of light shone against the wet stone walls, rainbows of color flickering. She heard crackling and grinding all around her.

"Shield your eyes, Morgan. The light may be too bright for a moment. But again, have no fear," the voice said, and she obeyed, though she had no idea why. With her eyes shut tight, the cracking sound was louder, bouncing against the jagged edges of her prison walls.

And then it stopped. As quickly as it had started, the sound was gone, and Morgan heard the ocean's soft roar from the cave mouth again. She risked opening her eyes, just barely under her lashes, to see what had happened and the crystal wall was gone.

Not far from her stood a tall man, with dark hair and dark burgundy cloak around him. She could feel the magic around him immediately. He was a powerful sorcerer.

"There, that is much better, isn't it. Now we can meet properly. My name is Mordred. I am of the Unseelie Court, and I am at your service." He gave a flourished bow, smiling broadly as he raised his head.

"You said you are from my mother's people, but my mother was not of the Unseelie Court." It was all she could think to say in response. Morgan knew her mother was one of the Fae - one of the shining ones who were not mortal. Merlin had told her this, but he never said she was a member of the dark Fae royal court.

"Merlin did not know. There are, believe it or not, a few things that your father does not know. Your mother didn't tell him, but she was of royal blood in our world. She was High Born and a beloved of the Unseelie Queen. Her love for Merlin drew her from us. We know how that ended for her, sadly," Mordred said, taking a few steps closer to Morgan.

"What do you want, Sir?" Her head was spinning, and she needed to be away from the cave, from this man, from the questions that were rattling around her skull.

"Let's not be so formal, Morgan. Call me Mordred. We shall be great friends, of this I am certain. What I want is only to help you, as a member of our court by blood. I want to help you now and in the future. Together, we have the means to craft whatever it is you wish.

You need only ask." He stepped closer again, and now, in the light of the candle, she could see that his skin had a sheen like a pearl.

"I wish to leave this cave, to go help my friend before it is too late." He took another step closer, standing between her and the path out into the morning light.

"I fear the Lady Igraine has already been played the fool. Merlin's trick worked. She carries the Pendragon seed now. But something else has happened that Merlin did not intend; Pendragon is dead." There was now scarcely an arm's length of space between them. The scent of raspberries and rich cream swirled around Morgan, heady and intoxicating.

"But that will mean war with his kingdom. Who would do such a thing?" She could imagine Merlin pacing with his injured leg, trying to solve a problem he had not foreseen. *How had such a thing escaped his gaze?*

"Morgan, you have questions, and I will answer them all for you in due time. Have faith that I am your ally, your true friend. Trust me, my *deirfiúr*. But first things first, let's leave this place and go to our rath for a proper homecoming. We'll set things right in Tintagel, have no fear."

He reached out that pearlescent hand of his, palm open, waiting for her to take it. The sound of the sea echoed down the cave, calling for her to leave. His eyes had a dark burgundy glow to them, matching his cloak. They looked at Morgan with a merry gaze, nothing giving away their secrets.

"And you'll tell me everything, no secrets?" She let her hand hover above his, waiting for his response.

"There is nothing you shall not know. Our plans, our magic - all given freely to you, ready for you to wield." He smiled, and she felt her hand touch his palm. The magic in his skin radiated against her, and he closed his fingers around her in a clasp.

"Let's begin, Morgan."

CHAPTER NINETEEN

Igraine woke with a soldier's arms supporting her as Ithyl dragged Arthur toward the cells, that were little hovels kept for the few who dared to break the law around Tintagel. They were isolated, behind the stables, near the edge of the sea. *That's where Ithyl was taking Arthur for the death of Uther Pendragon.*

"Are you alright, Lady?" The soldier asked, kindly, and in a low voice. He felt solid against her when everything else felt like a bad dream.

"Yes, I am alright. Do you know why Lord Ithyl has taken Arthur Spear for this crime? On what evidence?" Igraine turned to watch the young soldier's face. He looked barely older than Arthur himself.

"Lord Ithyl found the bloody blade with the scoundrel. He also had a bag of the Prince's jewels on his person. A common thief," The soldier spat on the ground, too close to her shoes for her liking. *Arthur with Uther's jewels? It doesn't make any sense at all.*

"Please tell Lord Ithyl that I must speak with him. I'll meet him in the Great Hall," Igraine said before turning toward the landbridge and the path to *The Gloria* in the small harbor. Someone had to have proof that Arthur didn't do this terrible crime, and Igraine was determined to find it.

It seemed all of Tintagel knew what had happened, despite Merlin's wish for secrecy. Ithyl hadn't been subtle in his search for Arthur, and everyone she passed on her way to the ship was gossiping about Arthur and the murder. She could only imagine how upset Edith would be when she heard the news. *I'll have to go check on her as soon as I can. But first, I need to find some kind of proof to save Arthur from death, because death will be the only punishment for the crime of murder.*

The ship was there, still bobbing in the harbor, though Igraine saw her sailors scurrying about to prepare to sail. They weren't going to wait for their shipmate; *The Gloria* would leave Tintagel as soon as the tide permitted. *Perhaps they worry they are next for the cells if they don't go now.* Ithyl hadn't left any guards to keep them in place.

She spied Hereca carrying a heavy basket loaded with spring onions, making her way to the ship. Hereca wore sailor's breeches, and her usual headscarf wrapped tightly around her dark hair. Around her waist, she wore a short sword.

"Hereca, wait, please," Igraine called, finding it hard to run on the rocky beach. The stones were slippery from the waves, and they rolled under her feet.

"Lady, why are you here?" Hereca put the basket down and placed her hands on her hips, looking as stern as she'd ever seen her.

"Arthur, he's been taken." Igraine said, to which she nodded.

"Yes, we saw it happen. The king's brother says Arthur murdered someone. It never happened." Her face held nothing but anger, and she was aiming it at Igraine.

"You must help me prove his innocence. He'll die if we don't save him!" Again, the pirate nodded.

"Yes, he'll die. There is nothing I can do to save him, though. Lord Ithyl says he found jewels and a knife on Arthur, clear evidence of his crime. The word of a pirate woman will mean nothing to them."

"Hereca, please, come with me. We must try to help him. How do you know he is innocent? Tell me that, and we can then go tell Lord Ithyl." Her feet kept shifting on the slippery rocks as she fidgeted. *The longer we wait down here, the less time we have.*

"Lady, I know Arthur loves you, and I know that love has brought him to this place. He should never have come back here. Your pledge to marry that prince, it broke him. But he couldn't have done this, even if his heart were willing to, he couldn't have because he was here, on the ship, with me, all night." Her eyes narrowed, glowering at Igraine. Eyes that blamed her for Arthur's fate.

"What do you mean by that? He wasn't here on the ship all night, surely."

"I said what I meant. Arthur was here, on the ship, with me. In my bunk until after sunrise. He never left me." She leaned down to pick up her basket again. "He needed comfort, and I wanted companionship. It was nothing more than that. But your Lord Ithyl won't take the word of a pirate that he was sharing her bed as proof."

"Hereca, that is impossible because Arthur was with me last night!" The words were out of Igraine's mouth before she could stop them. Hereca shook her head, though Igraine couldn't tell if it was in amusement or pity because her face betrayed nothing.

"Lady, I don't know who you slept with last night, but I promise you, it wasn't Arthur."

♛

EVERY STEP UP the cliffside path felt impossible as if Igraine were trudging through deep mud. Step after step, slogging along the way with the weight of Hereca's words binding her to the ground.

It wasn't possible. Hereca had to be lying, trying to give Arthur a claim to protect him from Ithyl. *But if that were true, why wasn't she trying to help? I could bring her before the king and give her that chance, but instead, she's preparing to set sail and leave Arthur in his cell. Why lie and do nothing?* It made no sense to Igraine.

Was it possible that after Arthur left me, he went to the ship and was with Hereca? Could she be mistaken about him being aboard all night? Maybe she just thought he was on the boat all night but only saw him for a few hours? If that were true, other sailors aboard the ship would have seen him come, and they could tell their story to Ithyl.

"By the thunder of Taranis, what is happening?" Igraine shouted as she reached the clifftop and stared at the castle walls across the landbridge. She needed a seer, she needed someone who could tell me the truth of what was happening. She needed Morgan.

Igraine hurried across the path, shoving aside the steady stream of people going about their daily business, oblivious to the nightmare around them. *She hadn't seen Morgan since early yesterday, she thought, or perhaps the day before.* For certain though, Igraine knew Morgan wasn't at Merlin's side this morning, which was a rare thing.

The Great Hall was bustling, as usual, when she came in from the morning light outside. Her father's throne was empty; he must be in his privy chamber, planning for defense against Ceredigion's wrath once they learned of the death of their prince. Igraine planned to check Merlin's room first to see if the old sorcerer was there or perched near her father's shoulder.

"Lady, a message for you, from Edith. She asks you to come to her quickly," Gisela said as she hurried over to her mistress, out of breath.

"Gisela, please tell Edith I will be there directly. I must first find the Lady Morgan. But I will be there. Please tell her." With a nod, Gisela ran back toward the door.

She pressed on through the room, heading up the stairs to the royal chambers above. She wondered if Uther's body was still lying on the bed or if they were preparing it for the journey home, washing away the blood, and dressing him in a fine shirt. *A finely dressed corpse borne home with the man who was supposed to have killed him.*

"Stop it," Igraine muttered, telling herself to push the thoughts from her mind. She couldn't let herself get drawn into the dark images that were hovering. If she was going to be of any use to Arthur, she had to keep her mind focused on clearing his name.

Igraine reached the sorcerer's door and rapped loudly with her fist on the hard oak. She heard a scuffle of feet from within, and impatiently she waited for him to reach the threshold.

"Igraine, what can I do for you?" He looked much paler than he had seemed that morning.

"Merlin, I am looking for Morgan, I must speak with her. Do you know where she is?" The old man gave her a strange look and ushered her into his room. She would have preferred to stay where she was, but he wasn't going to speak until she joined him.

"Why are you looking for my daughter?" He motioned for her to sit near the fireplace, which he had banked to a roaring blaze. The room was stifling.

"I need a seer, I need her to tell me the truth of something I have learned." There was no point in making up stories; he'd see through anything she might say anyway, and Igraine was long past caring what he thought of her.

"You seek a seer, and yet you think of my daughter and not myself? That is amusing." He spoke in a soft, chuckling voice, which puzzled her. Usually, the proud Merlin wasn't one to accept a slight from anyone.

"I mean no offense, Merlin. It is just that the matter is delicate, and I wished to inquire with someone..."

"Someone that you like and trust. I understand, Lady Igraine. You and I have not always seen eye to eye. I know you have disagreed with me on many things. It is natural you would wish to speak with Morgan rather than me. Unfortunately, Morgan is not here and cannot help you." He sat, leaving her standing. No other courtier would sit in the presence of Igraine or her father.

"Where is she?"

"She is away, for now. I hope for her return, but it will likely be a while before we see her again. But I can assist you, Lady. You wish for me to see whether Arthur killed Uther, is that not so?" Apparently, word of Arthur's arrest had reached the sorcerer's chamber.

"Yes and..." Igraine paused, not wanting to say what was almost as important to her. *Had Arthur spent the night with Hereca as she claimed? How could he be in two places?*

"What else, Igraine? If I am to help you, I must know all." He tented his fingers together, forming a long, thin pyramid pointing under his beard. For the first time, Igraine noticed his eyes were a gray-blue color.

"I know you owe your allegiance to my father, but what I tell you now, I ask that you keep to yourself. I know Arthur Spear did not do this thing because he was in my bedchamber last night. And yet…a sailor on his ship claims he was with her all last night. Both things cannot be true." Igraine expected some look of surprise or disapproval or anger on Merlin's face, but instead, he looked at her kindly.

"Lady, there are things that happen that seem impossible, and yet they happen. Spring itself appears as a miracle from winter's death. Do not be so quick to disbelieve; just because you have no explanation for something, doesn't mean it can't happen."

"I trust my eyes, Merlin. I know Arthur was with me, and yet she claims he was with her. She has no reason to lie, so I must know the truth of it. Can you help me or not?" Her voice was louder now, but still, the old man smiled softly.

"Child, I can tell you I have already tried to see into the truth of Uther's death, and something is hiding the vision from me. Someone with powerful magic is keeping the truth away from my eyes. Whoever killed Uther, and I know it was not Arthur, they do not want to be found out."

"Then we must tell the king and Ithyl! We must save Arthur from being taken to Ceredigion with Uther's body." Igraine turned toward the door, but the sorcerer stayed in his seat.

"My Lady, the people of Ceredigion will demand blood for the death of their prince. If we do not send them a killer, they will take their revenge out against all the people of Dumnonia. The Veil is weakening and will not hold against both the men of Wessex and invaders from Ceredigion. If the Veil falls, the whole kingdom will fall." Merlin's soft smile finally had faded from his face, replaced instead with a look of profound sadness.

"So Arthur is to be sacrificed to save the Veil, to save the kingdom?"

"What choice do we have, Igraine?"

CHAPTER TWENTY

Morgan followed Mordred from the cave, stepping out into the bright sun and a face full of seaspray. She hadn't made up her mind if she was actually going to follow him to his rath. Morgan knew the stories as well as any child; lingering in the halls of the Fae was dangerous for any mortal. Even if her mother was Fae herself, what would it mean for her with her father's human blood in her veins, she wondered.

"I won't imprison you, Morgan. I would never do that to you. Your human father did that," Mordred said as if reading her thoughts. *Perhaps he had read them.*

"Why must I come to your rath, Mordred? You must understand my reluctance." The winds whipped her dark hair around her face like the snake tendrils of the Greeks' Medusa.

"It is a homecoming, and you should meet your kin. Queen Eithne wants to meet you. You should know your people because the Veil and its secrets belong to them. Have no fear, I will return you to this place unharmed." He turned toward the rocky cliff path that led back toward the hilltop, the backside of Tintagel visible in the distance. Whether she trusted him or not, she had her magic, and she would not be caught unaware. *Not again.*

"Lead on, Mordred."

♛

THE TWO HORSES waiting at the cliff rise bore them away from the castle, heading east, away from the shore. Whether the creatures were magic themselves or Mordred was casting a spell, she didn't know, but they crossed the land in a blur, as she clutched the reins in terror from the speed.

"I apologize for the haste, Lady, but I did not wish to delay," Mordred said, smoothing his burgundy cloak. Morgan could see now that there were tiny silver threads woven along the hem in a strange pattern, almost like the glyphs and signs she knew from her studies. *Yet, I cannot read them.*

"Welcome to our rath, *Dumha Draíochta*, the royal court of our Unseelie Queen Eithne. Follow me." He led her toward the squat mound of earth, studded with rocks and stones. Grazing sheep were only a stone's throw or so away.

"We are here?" She hoped that she didn't sound disappointed. She had expected a fairy fort to be hidden from the world, but she wondered if the queen and her court actually lived in a dirt mound. He laughed in reply and walked toward a small opening in the mound.

Mordred slipped into the dark crevasse, turning to beckon her to follow him. A bit stout as she was, it was a tight squeeze between the coarse stones; she felt her hair snag on the rough surface behind her. The last of the sunlight was behind them, and they stood facing the tiny dark tunnel.

"For you, I will light the path to the door. We can't have you tripping in the dark with those human eyes." From his pearlescent palm, a tiny flame, pale blue, danced before her eyes, shining a light on the tight space. Along the rock walls, Morgan could now see the same glyphs and signs on his cloak.

"Nearly there," he said merrily, but she didn't share in the mirth; Morgan detested small spaces. She kept her eye fixed on the light, calling in her mind to Lugh, god of light, to keep it burning. Mordred laughed again and stepped down the path.

After following his flame for several minutes, they stood in front of a large stone that completely blocked the path.

"We're here, Morgan. Now we must see if your mother's blood is strong in your veins. You must pass through the stone to the other side. I cannot do this for you. Only the *sídhe* can enter our royal rath."

"And how do I do this?" They were standing chest to chest, as he shifted to stand behind her, sliding along the tight tunnel that barely had space for them. She felt the smooth brocade of his cloak against her arm as he passed and saw the sheen of his face in the blue light.

"Place your palms on the stone and speak the words *'Is é mo chuid fola mo bhanna'*. Your blood is your bond to enter this place." He gave Morgan an encouraging nod, and she turned slightly to face the stone squarely. She could feel him standing right behind her, holding the light above her head.

The stones were rough against her fingers, but Morgan could feel the pattern carved across them this time. The symbols were etched across the surface, leaving nothing between them. The whole stones radiated power and protection. There was something enchanting this stone, warding anyone away who might try to touch it. It was all she could do to force her hands to stay still on the cold surface.

"Ignore the enchantment, that is your human blood feeling the warning. Focus on the call of your *sídhe* blood, and pass through."

She leaned into her palms and recited Mordred's phrase, closing her eyes to the dim blue light around her. She knew that she needed a clear mind and a strong focus on the stone if she were going to call any magic to her. Years of practice made it easy to focus solely on the ancient stone under her fingers. The glyphs seemed to crawl against her skin, moving and slithering as if alive to her touch. They were writhing, and she could almost hear a hissing sound as if they were snakes sweeping from a hidden burrow. She felt her hands start to fall, through the stone, but instead of jumping back, she focused on the words, chanting again. *My blood is my bond, my blood is my bond, my blood is my bond.*

Morgan stepped into a long hall, carved in rich gray marble. Hanging lanterns lined the space, sparking and sputtering with bright blue light. She felt Mordred behind her, and the swirl of his cloak came around to her left. *We are in the hall of the Queen of the Unseelie.*

"Well done, Morgan. I knew you had the power of your mother. Now we meet the queen."

Mordred led her down the hall, toward an opening that was lit with more of the strange blue light. She could hear voices, but she couldn't make out the words. Part of her wanted to turn back to the stone and push her way back into that dark tunnel, back to the land she knew. Her feet kept moving, urged on by the part of her that wanted to learn more about her mother and to meet the Fae queen.

They entered into a large throne room, with a ceiling that seemed to stretch on beyond sight. The walls were a pale blue crystal, reflecting that eerie light surrounding them, bathing them in a sea of sparkling blue prisms. Dozens of people were gathered before the dais of the queen, who sat on a wicker throne, twisted and curved, almost undulating underneath her slight frame. The people parted as Mordred led them forward.

"My Queen, as I promised, I bring you Aisling's daughter, Morgan," he said, as he swept a bow before the woman. Morgan followed his lead and also bowed, not sure what else she should do. When she looked up, she saw the queen looking at her with her head tilted to the side.

"Aisling's daughter. Yes, I see the resemblance, but there is too much of your father in your face," Queen Eithne said. A small wrinkle between her brows marred the ageless face. Her eyes were dark, like Morgan's own, but they had nothing else in common that she could see. Her black hair was braided as intricately as the weaving of her wicker throne.

"Still, your *sídhe* blood bonds you to our people, and I did so dearly love Aisling. We welcome you to our Court." She stood up, unfolding herself from the throne into her long height, and raised her arms in a proclamation.

"Courtiers of the Unseelie Court, I bid you welcome Morgan,

daughter of Aisling, beloved of the queen. In Morgan's honor, we will hold a grand *cèilidh* this night. Call the pipers and harpers, prepare the feast. Summon the hobgoblins, the sylphs, the spirits from the hills. The queen commands you make merry." To the roar of the courtiers, she sat again on her throne.

"I am honored, Majesty," Morgan said, speaking to her for the first time. Mordred nodded his approval.

"Morgan, I wished for our cousin to bring you to us because you must be told of the damage done by your father, Merlin, against our people. As heir to his blood, it falls to you to stop him. Will you listen to Mordred? I would hold no *sidhe* against their will." The queen's gaze was penetrating, staring into Morgan's eyes as if she were boring inside her. It was unnerving, and Morgan wanted to look away, but she didn't dare.

"Yes, of course, I will listen," she replied.

"You know that Merlin created the Veil to protect Dumnonia. What you may not know is he stole the magic he used from your mother, Aisling. Only *sidhe* magic could create the Veil, and Merlin, even as masterful as he may be, is only human. That magic, and the knowledge of how to perform it, belongs to our people, Morgan.

"If the Veil is allowed to stand, the *sidhe* will continue to suffer. We move about the unseen world, as is our birthright. The Veil interrupts this, creates a crack in our world, and drains our ability to remain hidden from the harmful eyes of humans. The longer the Veil remains, the weaker our protections. We cannot allow the Veil to stay." Mordred paused as he accepted a goblet from the page who brought them. Morgan took the silver goblet offered to her as well, but she wasn't ready to sip the wine.

"How can I help you with this problem? I cannot draw down the Veil. Only Merlin can do that." Morgan watched the queen and Mordred exchange a glance.

"The Veil is weaker, as I am sure your father has told you, but it holds true and will not fall, at least for now, unless we take action. Your father knew enough magic to cast the Veil over the human Kingdom of Dumnonia. Enough to keep it strong against the invaders from the east - Wessex, I believe they are called," the queen said before sipping from her own goblet. Morgan feared she would insult them if she didn't take a sip as well. She raised the goblet to her lips and felt the warmth of the wine as she drank. It was spiced with flavors she had never tasted.

"But, if another human kingdom were to also attack, the Veil would be strained, the magic weakened by keeping two armies at bay. When the Veil is weakened, it can then be confounded and the magic broken," Mordred said.

"I still don't understand," Morgan replied, feeling the soft effects of the wine on her head already. *How am I to play a part in this plan? What do they want of me?*

"Worry not, Morgan, all shall be explained to you. Your role is to help us bring forward the prophecy that returns the magic to its rightful place."

"I will not harm Merlin," she said, words rushing from her lips.

"We would not ask such a thing. Instead, you must bring the future son back to save his father, the king that will sit upon a united throne of England. The king must be saved by his own progeny." Queen Eithne's words made no sense to Morgan at all. *What son was she speaking of, and what king?* Both she and Mordred laughed lightly, smiling at Morgan.

"All shall make sense to you, dear Morgan. For now, let us feast and celebrate your homecoming. When it is time, you shall return to your world with all the answers you seek."

CHAPTER TWENTY-ONE

Igraine ran from Merlin's room, heading toward the cell that held Arthur. *Truth apparently didn't matter to anyone, she thought*; Arthur was the sacrifice to avoid war with Uther's people. Igraine knew she had to tell Ithyl; she felt sure that her uncle wouldn't let an innocent man pay with his life for this crime. *And what of Uther's real murderer?* There was no honor in letting him go free; surely, she reasoned, Ithyl would understand that.

Igraine shoved people from her path with apologies as she went. The distance from the turris to the stables never seemed so far before, in all the thousands of times she had walked the path, with Longshanks at her heels. Now, she couldn't tread the way fast enough.

Rounding the corner, Igraine saw a wagon hitched to two horses, with Ithyl's horse saddled nearby. Lying in the wagon, a figure wrapped in cloth and draped with a beautiful cloak, Uther's body prepared for traveling home.

"Where is Lord Ithyl?" She stopped at the guard who stood by the wagon.

"He brings the prisoner, and then we make haste for the road."

"Lady Igraine, help me," Edith said. Igraine hadn't seen her, sitting on a bale of hay on the other side of the wagon. She hurried over to her and embraced her. Her large frame shuddered in Igraine's arms.

"Oh, My Lady, they are going to take him to die. You must help me. They say he killed that prince, but you know he would never do that. Not our Arthur. Please, can you help him?" Her voice, cracked with pain and worry, brought tears to Igraine's eyes. The hurt of helplessness and fear were wracking her.

"Edith, I am going to speak with my uncle. I know Arthur didn't do this thing. I must make him believe me." Igraine gave her a tight squeeze and released her, feeling the woman's tears drip on her shoulder as she stepped back.

"Please," was all she said, trembling where she stood. From around the corner of the stables, Ithyl walked quickly, with Arthur behind him on a rope.

"Uncle, please wait," Igraine said, hurrying over to him. Arthur's face looked swollen as if someone had hit him. His shirt was smeared with mud, and the rope was tied around both wrists.

"Igraine, I do not have time, we must head north and make haste." Ithyl tried to push past her on the path to the rear of the wagon. Igraine heard the clammer of Ithyl's men assembling.

"Arthur is innocent. Merlin told me as much just now. You must wait and hear for yourself." Edith sobbed behind her, calling for her son. Igraine heard him whispering, "it will be fine, Ma" to soothe her.

"I have no time for the words of sorcerers. I found this man with proof of his crime. I need no more words than that. Move aside, girl or I shall move you myself." Ithyl's voice, never raised to her before, thundered in the air around them. Igraine could see how enemies on the battlefield would be afraid of him. His men called him the Rock for a reason.

"Uncle, I will not move until you listen to Merlin. He wants to sacrifice Arthur to save the kingdom from war. Where is the honor in that? We need to find the one who killed Uther!" Ithyl took a step toward her, still holding the rope that bound Arthur. Igraine saw Arthur try to pull back, to stop Ithyl's move toward her as if he could stop the large man's motion.

"Igraine, I don't want to hurt you, but you need to move now. Otherwise, I will call the guards to move you and hold you fast until we are gone. Do not make me do this, not to my brother's child." His words were now a rumbling whisper that only the few of them could hear. The crowd gathering behind the guards was quietly murmuring.

"Do what you must, Uncle, but I am not moving. Arthur is innocent."

Ithyl said nothing, but he nodded toward the guard who had been standing by the wagon. The man strode toward her and swept her into his arms, pinning her against him as she tried to pull away. Edith screamed, pulling at his arms, and another guard joined the fray and pushed the woman back against the hay, knocking her to the ground. Igraine heard Arthur roaring, screaming for him to stop. Her own screams rattled against the arms that held her against her will.

"Hold the princess until we are away. Try not to harm her. She has taken leave of her senses. Inform the king that we will make peace with Uther's people." Ithyl shoved Arthur into the wagon, even as he tried to kick at Ithyl. Another guard stepped forward and pinned him to the wagon floor as Ithyl secured his rope to the wagon wall. Arthur was prone, next to the body of the man he was accused of killing.

"There, that will hold you. Now, let's be off," Ithyl said, wiping the sweat from his brow and climbing into his saddle. The sounds of the horses and the wagon pulling away were muffled by Igraine's screams and Edith's sobs.

CHAPTER TWENTY-TWO

1984

Arty couldn't pay attention to Dr. O'Malley. The afternoon lectures and demonstrations were wasted on him. His mind was stuck at the top of the hill, at the little rock doorway where Lowen had pulled him into another world.

"Where are you at? Your mind isn't here," Elsbeth said as they started packing up for the bus ride back to the pub for the evening meal.

"Huh? Oh, yeah, right. Sorry, my mind is a bit scattered today," he mumbled, still feeling the damp socks sticking in his shoes.

"You might want to come back to earth because Dr. O'Malley noticed. She gave you quite a look," Elsbeth said, before heading off toward the exit. Arty had no idea what she was talking about.

"Mr. Drake, I do hope you weren't bored this afternoon," Dr. O'Malley said as he passed by her desk. From the scowl on her face, he could tell she wasn't pleased.

"My apologies, Doctor. I must have hit my head when I slipped in that wallow. I will do better tomorrow, I promise," he said.

"See that you do. If you've had a change of heart, we can give your spot to someone on the waiting list."

A change of heart. As he walked out into the brilliant sunshine, now hovering low to the west, the words rattled around his head. *Yes, I have had a change of heart - but not about the semester working; I don't want to go back through the portal.*

He had promised those two strange people, living in the little cottage, that he would go back and help the legendary Igraine - a woman right out of fiction. He had promised that he would go back and save not only his supposed ancestor but his whole family line. He had promised, and now, he wanted to take it all back.

"Arty, come on, Mum's waiting." Lowen sat on a picnic table near the training building, swinging her legs back and forth. The bus idled, filling the air with diesel fumes.

"Listen, Lowen," he said, walking toward her to keep anyone from hearing. The last thing he needed was someone overhearing him talking about this crazy stuff.

"She said you'd change your mind, that you'd try to back out, but I know you won't. Mum doesn't trust people, too many betrayals. But I know you'll do it. You gave your word." The imp with the orange hair smiled, and he noticed one of her teeth was missing, just like any other child her age.

"Lowen, I know I promised," he said, ready to say the words that would prove her wrong, but she bolted from the picnic table, racing ahead.

"Good, then come on. We have to hurry."

The bus honked, jolting him back from watching her bound into the hills. He walked over to the steps, and Mr. Dyer gave him a look; he was impatient to get going.

"You coming or not, Captain America?"

Arty hesitated, one hand on the railing and a foot raised to step into the bus. Something was stopping him; he felt it blocking him from taking that next step away from Tintagel.

"No, I am going to stay for a while. I'll walk back. Thanks, though."

"Suit yourself," he said, shaking his head as he shut the bus door. Arty turned to walk toward the little cottage.

♛

"He's here, Mum! I told you!" Arty heard Lowen's call as he rounded the bend and saw the garden again, this time with the light low behind the hillside.

"I'm coming, Lowen," her mother called from the cottage.

"What will I have to do?" Arty took a heavy seat on a wrought iron stool near the garden gate.

"We'll go back, just like we did this afternoon. But once you get there, you'll have to go on your own, I can't interfere. Mum says," Lowen replied, chasing a rather large moth as it flitted among the foxgloves.

"Arty, you'll be taken back to Tintagel, back to Igraine's time, and it will be night. You'll climb the rise, and she'll be on the cliffside. You need to stop her from stepping off the cliff. Once that is done, you'll go back to Lowen and come back. Does that make sense?" Morgan had come out from the house, carrying a large bowl in her hands. No small glass jar this time.

'How do I stop her? Won't she be terrified if some stranger comes toward her? She won't even understand modern English if I speak to her." *What in the world will I say to this person? I have no idea how this was going to work.*

"She will be startled, I suppose, but you must make sure she knows you mean no harm. Convince her not to jump from the cliff. My enchantment will allow you both to be understood. Tell her whatever you must, but do not tell her that I sent you back to save her. She must not know I am involved. Tell her it was Merlin if you like. Tell her whatever you want, just make sure she doesn't jump." She was walking slowly, making sure the liquid didn't slosh from her bowl. Lowen was still chasing the moth in the late afternoon sunshine.

"Arty, don't worry, it will be fine. Remember, Mum wouldn't send you if you couldn't do the job. Trust us," Lowen chimed in, and for some reason, her little voice made him feel better. She believed in him, he thought, that he could do this crazy thing. *If he could save someone's life, even a life from over a thousand years ago, wasn't it his duty to try?*

"Let's do this before I change my mind." Arty rose slowly from the chair. Lowen had the moth in her hands as she pranced around the flowers.

"Back to the doorway, Lowen," her mother said, and the girl released the moth before darting for the garden gate. The three of them walked up the hill, leading to the castle ruins.

"Close your eyes, Arty. Just hold my hand, and I'll pull you through like before. Because we are going way back, you might feel more of a pull this time. Don't be scared." Lowen lectured as her mother dipped a brush into the mixture in her bowl, painting the stones of the archway. Every edge of the stones was slick and dark.

"Just follow Lowen, and don't worry. Nothing is going to happen to you." Arty heard Morgan's voice, and Lowen squeezed his hand. His eyes were closed, but he could still see the light coming from over his shoulder in the west. *It must be almost time for it to dip below the horizon, he thought.*

Morgan was mumbling her words again, softly. They sounded like buzzing bees in his ears. Lowen started pulling on his hand, and Arty took a step forward. The archway was only another two steps away or so, but he still wanted to open his eyes and reach out a hand to brace against whatever was on the other side.

"Don't peek," the child said, seemingly knowing his thoughts. She pulled him forward, and he took the last few steps before he felt the pull, the tug on his arm that jerked him forward. He tried to say Lowen's name, but a blast of air kept the words from leaving his mouth. After a long moment, it was gone, and he felt the squeeze of her hand again.

"We're here," she whispered, and he opened his eyes. They were in the same doorway, only now it led to a garden, not too different from the one by the cottage. Arty swiveled his head to see the kitchen behind him.

"We're in the kitchen, away from the turris. Better to be clear of the guards. It's late, almost midnight. I'll lead you to the cliff edge, and then you go find Igraine. Okay?" She tugged his hand again, pulling him back into the kitchen, toward a door down the hall. From the corner of his eye, he saw something move.

"Don't worry, that is just Tân, the hobgoblin that lives here. He won't say nothing. I've been here before." Lowen led him along, even though they were walking in pitch darkness. Arty heard the soft squeak of the oak door as she pulled it open.

"Follow me and stay close. We don't have much time," Lowen said as she let loose of his hand and raced off into the night.

CHAPTER TWENTY-THREE

The guard finally let Igraine go, after Arthur and Ithyl were well out of sight. She could have jumped on a horse to pursue them, but she knew that she would never make it from the yard. Ithyl would have made sure of that.

"Oh, Lady, he's gone. I'll never see my boy again," Edith wailed from the hay bale, and though Igraine tried to soothe her the best she could, what was there to say. *It was likely she was right, now that Arthur was headed for Uther's lands and certain death.*

"Isn't there anything you can do? Lady, there must be something, some magic you know, some spell to stop them. You must save Arthur!" Edith pulled her sobbing shoulders away from Igraine, looking at her with eyes filled with anger. Igraine knew Edith wasn't angry at her, but the mother's anguish had to find release with someone.

"Edith, I'll try, I'll do whatever I can to save him." Igraine could tell that Edith wanted to believe her, but Edith knew as well as Igraine did that there wasn't much chance, not if they didn't get some help.

"Perhaps the crew can help, maybe the captain…" Igraine said, trying to make a list of possible allies. Morgan was nowhere to be found, Merlin wasn't going to help; there weren't many people left they could call on.

Igraine ran toward the landbridge, gazing over the cliff edge as soon as it came into sight. She wanted to find *The Gloria* still bobbing below, waiting to cast off on their trade mission. What she found instead was an empty bay. The ship and her crew were gone.

"Of course they are gone, no honor with pirates," Igraine yelled, startling the woman tending to a small flock of hens. The birds clucked at her to be quiet even if their mistress didn't dare to chide the princess.

My father. He is my last hope. Igraine could beg him to send a rider and force Ithyl to bring Arthur back to them. She had to persuade him. Surely he would see this for the terrible act that it was.

She sped back toward the turris, ready to beg her father for his help. Igraine told herself that she would marry anyone he said if it meant saving Arthur. *Whatever he needs for me to maintain the Veil, I'll do it, if only he will save him.*

"Lady, the king is not to be disturbed," the guard said as she stormed toward his privy chambers. Igraine saw another guard move his pike to bar the door.

"I will call down the fury of the Morrigan if you do not let me pass. Your livers will wither within you, I swear it, as a student of Merlin. Let me by!" Igraine bellowed, and both guards looked at each other in genuine fear. It might have amused her if she hadn't been seething with fury. *To think they are scared of my paltry magic.*

"Let her pass," the sorcerer said, opening the door. The guards moved their pikes, and Igraine marched past them with a glare.

"Igraine, have a care, would you? You scream like a harridan." Her father was sitting close to his fire, wrapped up in a wool shawl.

"I'll scream until the stones of Tintagel fall down around your ears if you don't listen to me, Father." Merlin chuckled lightly behind her as if this were amusing and not life and death.

"Calm yourself and speak clearly. I will listen but cease the shrieking. My ears are old and cannot bear it."

Igraine took a deep breath, ready to yell again, and then she stopped. *Nothing will be gained by pitching a fit. I have to convince him to see reason and to stop Ithyl. I need these old men on my side.*

"Apologies, Father, I am just distraught at the fate of Arthur Spear. He is an innocent man sent to die. That is not justice, Father."

"Daughter, I dare say he is not an innocent man; he sails with pirates, does he not? Why are you convinced he did not do this crime? Merlin believes him guilty." Igraine turned to look at the old sorcerer, and his eyes held no trace of his earlier words.

"Father, I know him innocent because... he was with me in my chamber last night. He could not have done this thing. Punish me if you must, but he is innocent." Telling Merlin this secret was one thing, but it cut her to her center to say it to her father. *As a princess of the realm, he could have me flogged for this, he could lock me in my rooms until the end of my days if that was his command.*

"Merlin, you will have to tell her. She won't listen to reason until you do." No wrath or surprise as Igraine might have expected. He was calm, speaking easily to his loyal sorcerer.

"Sire, do you think that is wise?"

"You must."

"Tell me what, Father?" Igraine couldn't stand watching them debate about her as if she weren't even there.

"Lady Igraine, we were not prepared to tell you this, not now, but Uther's death has forced our hand. We know you had a visitor last night, but it wasn't Arthur Spear." Igraine started to protest, to stammer her refusal of this, but Merlin held up a gnarled hand to silence her.

"It wasn't Arthur Spear, it was Uther Pendragon, enchanted to look like Arthur by my magic. It was to ensure that the child of prophecy was conceived. You broke your word to marry Uther, so we had to...take measures."

Igraine heard him, the words said in his raspy voice, but they were meaningless to her. *Arthur, in my bed just last night, was not Arthur at all.* Uther, who had seemed a decent man, had been in disguise, pretending to be Arthur. And her father, and Uther, and Merlin had all agreed to this plan.

"It cannot be. You wouldn't do that to me, Father. No, you lie."

Revulsion filled her gullet. The words finally piercing her skull. The blue robe, the one Arthur had been wearing, the robe that belonged to Uther. Hereca's claim that Arthur had been with her all night. Those smooth, soft hands that had lifted her shift over her head.

"No, no, how could you do that?" Igraine's voice choked as she sank into a chair. The old men exchanged worried looks.

"We had no choice, Igraine. You left us with no choice. Uther did not know either if that is a comfort. We had to have you fulfill the prophecy. It was the only way," her father said, leaning forward from his chair. She could smell the gooseberries he had just eaten on his breath and his shawl's musty smell. He reached out a hand toward her, and she recoiled.

"Igraine, you carry Uther's child. Now that he is dead, this child will be heir to his kingdom. This child will unite our lands and keep everyone safe. This child, *your* child, must be born." Merlin spoke to her, softly and calming as if she were some skittish broodmare. The sound of his voice made her skin crawl, and she wanted to claw his eyes out with her trembling hands.

"You have done a hateful, monstrous thing, and the Morrigan curse you for it. The treachery of both my teacher and my father is beyond bearing. How can I ever forgive you for this?" Igraine knew that she had to leave the room, the disgusting smells and sounds, the heat from that damn fire, the very air these two creatures were breathing. *I have to get out of here.* She stood up, knocking the chair behind her and turning for the door.

"Wait," her father said, but Merlin raised his hand again. Igraine left them both behind as she slammed the oak door behind her.

CHAPTER TWENTY-FOUR

Arthur and I were pawns in a game. He will be sacrificed to save the peace, and I have been tricked into that bed, by men who are supposed to protect me. Cruelly used so I can fulfill some damn prophecy.

"Lady, you must eat something, you haven't stirred from your chair all day." Gisela fussed over Igraine, bringing her trays to tempt her to eat, but Igraine wouldn't be soothed. By the shadows on the wall, it was near dusk. She hadn't risen from the chair by the window all day, keeping the bed behind her because she couldn't bear to look at it.

Daylight dwindled, and soon Gisela was lighting candles for her, unasked. Igraine hadn't spoken a word to her all day, which she knew was unkind, but she couldn't get words to leave her lips. *If I say anything, I might say everything, and I am not ready to do that.*

"Lady, I know you fear for young master Spear, but you must trust that things will work out as the gods will it. Keep faith that things will be alright." Igraine's reply pressed against her teeth, ready to spew forth on the one person who cared about her most in the wretched place. *If the gods were behind what had happened to Arthur and me, maybe it is time for me to forsake them.*

Igraine said nothing, just nodding so Gisela would leave. Igraine wouldn't hurt her, not with her rage, for something Gisela had no control over. Igraine knew too well being used against one's will. The night deepened, and the flickering light burned into her eyes as she stared into the flame. *How easy to snuff the candle, to take the light from the world.*

She stood before she knew what she meant to do. Igraine snatched a cloak from the wall and left her room, the candles still burning as if she were yet melted into her chair. It wouldn't be long before Gisela came to check on her again.

Down the halls with her hood pulled over her head, Igraine snuck along until she found the crisp night air outside the castle. She made her way toward the kitchens, the last building before the rise of the cliff overlooking the sea. Igraine had promised Edith that she would help and do everything to save Arthur, but she had failed her. Igraine couldn't face her now, knowing the truth and unable to save her son.

The wind blew hard against her as if trying to push her from the cliffside. The moon lit the path, and Igraine pressed on, feeling the rocky slope with each step beneath her thin slippers. It would have been a gorgeous scene on any other night, with the waves lapping at the rocks and the light reflecting on every swell.

"Damn them all, I won't be used," she said to the wind that blew back her hood and blew the strands of hair from her face.

"Daughter of Tintagel, I hear you there," a voice replied, and she nearly slipped as she jumped at the sound. The voice was coming from somewhere below her.

For a moment, Igraine wondered if maybe Gisela was on the path down the cliff, the way the fishermen use to cast nets. Almost as soon as she thought of it, she dismissed it; Gisela was far too old to follow that craggy path. The voice didn't sound like her, it sounded almost like a song.

"This is not your destiny," the voice sang, sounding beautiful and pleading at the same time. *How could I have thought this was Gisela?* Igraine knew from songs and stories that selkies lived in these waters. It had to be one of the beings of the sea.

"This wasn't my destiny, either," Igraine shouted back, pulling her hand back from her stomach, where she had been clutching it. "I choose my fate, not them, not you."

"Your life is still your own. Choose your own destiny, Igraine. Do not let others decide for you. If you join us, nothing you dreamed of will come to pass. Be strong and live."

The sound of footfall on the path turned her head. She thought that it had to be a guard sent by her father or perhaps even Gisela herself, worried that Igraine wasn't where she had left her. Instead, Igraine saw a man in strange clothing, coming toward her from the rise of the cliff.

"What do you want? Who are you?" Igraine called out. He said nothing.

"I said, who are you? Answer me." She might be afraid, but she was still a princess of this kingdom, and she would stand brave before him.

"Are you Igraine? Please don't jump. My name is Arthur," the man said, slowing his step as he held his hand out toward her.

"Stay away from me. Do not approach me." Igraine called back, knowing how close she was to the cliff edge that was now at her back.

"I won't, I promise, but please, step back from the edge. You can't fall, please." He was waving his hand as if to beckon her closer.

"Whether I stand or fall is of no concern to you. Leave me in peace."

"No, Princess, you must not do that. If you jump, you'll...kill me." He looked terrified, standing on the path as if he were about to fall into the sea.

"Speak sense, man. Nothing shall harm you, whether I step from this hill or not." *Again, another man to tell me what I can do, what I should do. A stranger with no right at all.*

"Listen, I know this sounds unbelievable, but please listen to me. I know that you are...with child, and I know you were tricked. I also know that the baby must live because he is my ancestor. If he dies, my whole family line dies with him. So please, step back from the edge."

Igraine stared at him. She was sure that he had to be some kind of sorcerer, some kind of magician who could know something she had only learned herself just that day. *Some sort of trickster in human form come to fool me, surely.*

"You cannot know that," Igraine said, feeling wobbly in her knees. The ground felt slippery beneath her feet.

"But I do know it, and I am here to save you from doing what you are thinking of doing. Your child is important, not just to my family, but to your whole country." The man had taken another step toward her, and she threw out her arms to halt him. *Whatever magic he had planned, she thought, he wasn't going to get close.*

"Oh yes, I know how important this child is to this realm. Some prophecy that Merlin has called down on me, a prophecy that requires I carry this child. I won't be used, Sorcerer, by him or by anyone else."

"Sorcerer? Me? No, I'm no sorcerer, I am just Arthur - Arty, my family calls me. My father is Archie, and my granddad, he was Arthur also. For as far back as anyone remembers, men in my family were called Arthur or Arty. I'm not magic, but I was sent here to save you." The man stepped backward, again beckoning her to join him away from the cliffside. Igraine heard a voice on the wind say, "hurry up"; the voice sounded like a child.

"You don't save me, stranger. I am through with men making choices for me. If I am to be saved, as you say, I save myself. I make my choices, not you, not my father, not Merlin, not anyone."

"Then make a choice to save my family, to save me. And maybe, there is a way to save Arthur - *your* Arthur - from his fate. But you'll never know if you jump." He stepped backward again, and this time, Igraine stepped toward him. *Could this stranger be able to help me save Arthur?*

"How would you save him?" Igraine called to him, as he took another step back, his arm still beckoning. She followed with another two steps, leaving the cliff behind her.

"I don't know, but I will find out, and I will come back with a plan. I promise you. Just trust me, okay?" With another step, he turned and hurried down the path, leaving her alone on the cliffside. Again she heard a child's voice as she stepped toward the way back to the castle.

"What have you done?" The small voice faded before Igraine reached the rocky edge. The man, whoever he was, was gone.

CHAPTER TWENTY-FIVE

1984

"What have you done?" Lowen asked Arty again, this time as they were standing by the ruins of the doorway at Tintagel. Morgan was there, and it was bright daylight. They were back.

"Lowen, what happened?" Her mother didn't ask Arty. *Funny that she wants a report from a child, not the adult.*

"He did it, he saved her, but..."

"I promised to save Arthur, err...her Arthur. And I meant it." Morgan turned to look at Arty as he spoke, and he couldn't tell if she was shocked or annoyed or both.

"Arthur Spear is irrelevant. He wasn't the reason we sent you back."

"He's a person, someone who needs help and helping him was the only way I could convince Igraine to listen to me. You said to do whatever it takes to save her. I did that."

Morgan was quiet, mulling over his words, watching Lowen as she shook her head in disagreement.

"Your promise is likely impossible to fulfill, you know that, yes? He was sent with the king's brother as atonement for Uther's murder.

By saving him, you could cost others their lives in a war. Nothing is just a single act, everything has consequences and impacts the fate of others. Do you understand that?" She spoke without a lecturing tone, just plainly and earnestly. Arty could tell she wanted him to know the full weight of what he had done. And he did know. Saving Arthur was the right thing to do, he was sure of it.

"Yes, I understand. You lived then, Morgan. Was the war with Uther's kingdom prevented because of Arthur's sacrifice?"

"I...can't recall. It was a long time ago." Morgan turned away from him, gazing out over the water. He knew she was lying.

"Look, I know that I can't keep this promise without your help. But I think we should save Arthur. He might not be my ancestor, but I don't think it was right what happened to him. Will you help me keep my word?"

Morgan watched the waves, lost in her own thoughts, and Arty knew he'd have to just wait for her to finish wrestling with herself and make her decision. Lowen had scampered off, strangely silent on the matter. Whatever decision was made, it would be Morgan's alone.

"Alright. Perhaps we can help Arthur. There are things I've done in the past that I regret. Maybe this helps make up for some of that. The question now is, how do we save Arthur? It won't be something you can do alone. I'll have to go back with you."

She finally turned back toward Arty, and he saw the worry on her face. *What had Lowen said about the effects of going back in time, that it aged you? If Morgan was already thirteen hundred years old, how would that hurt her?* There had to be more about this that he didn't know.

"What do you need me to do?" Arty followed her down the hillside, back toward the cottage.

"Help me convince Lowen. She's going to be furious."

"So, what now?" Arty asked, back in the cottage with the sullen Lowen eating cookies as fast as she could grab them off the plate. In between bites, she'd look over at Arty with menace in her eyes.

"Now, you and I go back and find Ithyl on the road, before he makes it back to Uther's kingdom. We'll rescue Arthur and then return back to this time. When that is done, assuming we are successful, you can go back to your life." Morgan was mixing more herbs into her bowl, preparing another mixture to streak across the stone archway. Arty hadn't noticed the streaks of silver in her dark black braid before.

"And that's it? That's all?" Arty asked, feeling like there was something he was missing. *We'll just let him go, and then what? I'll never know what happens to Arthur Spear or Igraine.*

"That's enough, Arty. I have my doubts we can even pull this off. But if we do, then yes, that's it. You get to be a student again and out of all this. That should please you." She looked over her shoulder and gave him a small smile.

"Yes, I suppose so," Arty muttered, glancing down at the brooding child seated across from him. She gave her head a small, warning shake. Arty needed a minute alone.

"May I use your facilities?" Arty asked, standing from the table. Morgan gave him a confused look until Lowen spoke through her cookie-filled teeth.

"He means the WC, Mum."

"Oh, certainly, just through there," she gestured, pointing to a small door he hadn't noticed before. He bent to enter the tiny room through the short archway and closed the door behind him.

The bathroom was barely bigger than the one on the airplane to England. He turned on the cold tap, splashing water on his face. His eyes felt tired, and he glanced into the mirror hanging on a rusty nail. Staring back at him was his face, with a streak of white hair flopping on his forehead. He gave it a tug, twirling the strands in his wet fingers. It hadn't been there that morning.

"Uh, Morgan, what's happened to me?" Arty called as he left the tiny room, wiping his wet hands on his shirt.

"He means his hair, Mum." Lowen said, this time without the cookie filter.

"What? Oh, the streak of silver. We did say that going through the portal would age you. Do you remember? Now, where did I put that mugwort jar?" Morgan squatted to search a low cupboard.

"And he wants to go back again," the girl chimed in, sounding smug.

"Don't listen to her, Arty. Nothing wrong with a few gray hairs. But...I would say this should be your last trip back." She found the jar and stood, giving a little grunt once her knees were straightened. "You should eat something because we're going to go soon."

♛

Lowen had stayed back at the cottage, at Morgan's insistence. Arty didn't ask why but he could guess there was some fear she'd follow them through the portal. Arty could tell Morgan wanted to make this a quick trip.

"The portal doorway is in Tintagel, as you know. We'll have to make our way north on the road and catch up with Ithyl. I can cast a spell to make it easier for people to ignore us, but we need to stay away from the castle residents as much as we can. I'm sending us back to just after Arthur leaves with Ithyl, so we have a chance to catch them." Morgan brushed the stones as she spoke, slicking them with her potion of herbs, and Arty had no idea what else. The sun dipped below the horizon, and it was getting dark.

"Why don't we just go back to before Ithyl catches Arthur and warn him?"

"We can't do that. Too much meddling in the events of the time will change the future, and that might mean ripple into our own time, here and now. The less we change things, the better. Ithyl must believe he has captured Arthur, or he could tear up the castle looking for him or, worse yet, get Merlin involved. No, we need to free Arthur on the road." She placed the empty bowl on the stone wall and stood in front of the ruined doorway, with her left hand outstretched toward Arty.

Without replying, he stepped forward and clasped it, ready to walk through the portal again.

"Stay close to me, Arty. I can't protect you if you are far away." He heard her words as she stepped forward, pulling his arm, and she walked into the portal. The painful tug yanked him forward, and the gush of wind kept any answer he might make out of his mouth.

Another tug and he was back in the kitchen doorway of Tintagel, with Morgan still holding his hand. This time, the kitchen was abuzz with people, all hustling around as they prepared some meal. Not one of them looked toward them.

Arty didn't dare speak but instead, let Morgan pull him through the hallway, the same one that Lowen and Arty had traveled to get out to the path they had followed to the cliffside. Not one of the women working looked up from their chores.

Out in the open air again, she pulled Arty to the right and then left, toward a stable area. He could smell the horse dung in the warm air, and someone was pounding on metal, making a clank-clank noise. *Did they have horseshoes in the late 600s?* Arty would have to ask Morgan, but it would have to wait until they were away from the castle.

Morgan dropped her hand once they were near a stall where a horse was tied, munching easily on some hay. The stable hands were not nearby, but still, she leaned over to whisper.

"We'll take one horse and ride together. With any luck, we'll catch up to Ithyl's party since they are hauling a wagon and will be moving slower. I hope you can ride." She placed the bridle and saddle on the horse as easily as she had mixed her potion. She was on top of the horse in a matter of moments.

"I don't know about riding, but I can hang on," Arty whispered as he hopped onto a stump, using it as a platform to get on the horse's back. After a moment of panic and a quick grip of her waist, he was on the horse, clamping his thighs around its round middle.

"Hold on," she said, giving the stirrups a little tap against the horse's sides. She walked the horse from the stables, slowly moving away from the direction where Arty had found Igraine. This time, they were headed east, toward the land bridge that led to the hillside. Wagon tracks rutted the soft dirt in front of them.

They crossed the bridge, with Arty squinting, his eyes closed as much as he dared over the high and narrow path, and then Morgan gave the horse the command to run. Arty clutched her for dear life, feeling the horse bouncing below him, with only the strength of his legs holding him on. *This is probably the most terrifying thing I have done, and that includes traveling through time, he thought.* Arty was sure that he would be landing on some boulder at any moment, cracking his head wide open, never to be seen again by his family.

"Arty, can you loosen your grip a little? I can't breathe," Morgan said, and he let his arms relax a fraction. She slowed the horse's pace a bit as they crested over a small hill before pulling to a stop. Arty was never so grateful to be standing still.

"See that, there in the distance? That's Ithyl's party." She pointed to some figures far ahead on the road, dust plumes making them even harder to see. "We need them to stop so we can catch up and get Arthur."

They were hardly more than a few miles from the castle. Why would Ithyl need to stop so soon, Arty wondered. *Surely, they'd keep riding until dusk.* Arty was about to say so out loud when he heard Morgan muttering words that he didn't know.

"*Briseadh an roth, briseadh an roth, biotáillí na talún, briseadh an roth,*" she chanted. After a few moments, she stopped, and he felt her take a deep breath of air.

"That should do it," she said, nudging the horse forward.

"What was that?"

"I asked the spirits of the earth to break one of their wheels. That should give us the time we need."

♛

ONCE THEY WERE CLOSE ENOUGH to the group of men to be seen, Morgan left the road, riding close enough to them yet keeping under the cover of some scrub brush. She pulled the horse to a stop and slid from the saddle, leaving Arty to fumble down with a thump. He had no idea how he would get back up on the horse again, but he was glad to have the solid dirt under his feet.

"To fix the wagon, they'll pull Arthur and Uther's body out, and that's when we'll set him free. I'll cause a little distraction to be sure they are occupied. You take this knife and free Arthur. Tell him to stay out of sight and get as far from the castle as he can. Don't waste time though, we won't have much of it before someone might come looking for him." Morgan had pulled a small knife from the bag she had slung across her shoulders. She passed the blade to Arty, pulling it out of the sheath.

"Whatever you do, don't tell him about me."

Arty took the knife and turned toward the grouping that was just on the other side of the small hedge. From between the brambles, he could see men dragging two bodies from the wagon - one wrapped in cloth and the other bloody and bound. Arthur's red hair stood out in the sun. The soldiers were so close, he could smell the sweat coming off them. *Whatever Morgan had planned for her distraction, she'd have to make it a good one, he thought. Even if she does have that spell that keeps us hidden.* Before Arty could turn back to ask her what she had planned, he heard a loud yell.

"Lord Ithyl, look!" A man yelled, and he heard rustling and clanging as they ran from the lop-sided wagon. Arty scurried over to the hedge's edge and saw a blast of fire crackling on a tree at the edge of the road. With a mighty crack, the tree fell, blocking the road completely.

"It will set the whole road ablaze if we don't stomp it out," a man shouted, sliding down from the horse where he had been seated. From the look of his armor, Arty guessed the man was Ithyl. "Grab some blankets. Hurry."

"Now!" Morgan whispered, and Arty bolted from behind the hedge, hunching low to stay below the wagon's line. Arthur was only a few yards from Arty, awake but looking dazed.

"Who…" he started to say, but Arty shushed him and put the knife to the rope around his wrist and feet.

"There's no time. I came to rescue you, but you have to run, get away from here before those men find you are gone. Get as far from the wagon as you can." Arthur Spear rose from the ground, shaky and slow. *We don't have much time left, the fire is almost out.*

"Why…" Arthur asked as Arty helped pull him to his feet, tugging him to stay low.

"Because I promised Igraine. Now run!"

Arty shoved him forward, as gently as he could, watching him dash toward a gully on the roadside. He couldn't imagine that he would make it very far when Ithyl discovered that he was gone. Arthur didn't have a horse or any way to outrun them and he was badly beaten. Arty hoped that Morgan had thought of that.

Back around the corner of the brambles, Morgan was back in the saddle, offering Arty an arm to help hoist him up. He found the empty stirrup and let her help haul him onto the horse's back before they turned and galloped from the road.

"They'll catch him," Arty huffed, still catching his breath.

"No they won't. Arthur has the same enchantment that we had in Tintagel. It will last long enough for him to make enough distance to get free. After that, he'll have to use his wits to stay safe, but you honored your word to Igraine. Let's get back to the castle and back through the portal."

CHAPTER TWENTY-SIX

Morgan knew she had drunk too much wine; she could feel her head swimming. The Fae queen's servants kept filling her goblet, and she was too busy listening to the harp music to notice. *Even the great feasts at Tintagel paled in comparison to the banquet given in her honor.*

"You are having a good time, yes?" Mordred asked, sitting across the table from her. She could barely hear him over the music.

"Oh, yes, it is wonderful. I am so honored." Morgan thought that she might be shouting, but she couldn't be sure in her drunken state. Mordred chuckled at her.

"Might I peel you from the celebration so we can discuss the plan regarding the Veil?" She nodded in reply though truthfully, now was probably not the best time to be making any decisions, not with the wine in command.

"Lead on," she said, rising carefully from the table. Mordred stood as well and took her hand to lead her from the raucous hall, down a quieter path to a small receiving room. He shut the door behind them, and she marveled at the quiet.

"There, that is better. We don't want to forget the true reason for your visit. We must discuss the Veil and its destruction. We need your assistance, Morgan." Morgan had taken a seat, but Mordred decided to lean against a heavy table, one leg lifted against the edge. For the first time, she noticed that his trousers were the same deep burgundy as that cloak of his.

"As we discussed, your father...errr...Merlin's use of our magic created the Veil, but it harms our people by its very existence. We need to draw down the Veil to restore balance. The only way to do that is to ensure that the prophecy involving Igraine's human child does not fulfill his destiny. You must ensure this does not happen, that is your role to play." He had picked up a small crystal resting on the table, a lovely shade of pale pink, and he tossed it between his hands as he spoke. The light glinted off the crystal gently, and she couldn't keep her eyes from it.

"I won't hurt Igraine or her child, you must know that," Morgan said, sounding stern to her ears.

"We would not ask you to. You must keep Igraine from allowing Merlin to take her child. If Merlin raises that child, he will fulfill his destiny and become the king of all England. A legendary king and one who will change the fate of the world. Dumnonia would remain hidden from memory. Her people kept within their world, safe but moving through time without change, without new faces or experiences. And not to mention the harm this does to the Fae world." He gently placed the crystal back on the table and rose from his resting spot, stepping closer to her. She could smell the raspberries and cream again, the scent that came from him as he stood hovering.

"So, what do you ask of me?" Morgan craned her neck, looking at him as he smiled down on her.

"Tonight or when we return to Tintagel tomorrow?" He smiled broadly. He reached his hands out, and she lifted her own to clasp them. Mordred pulled her lightly from the chair, with scarcely a whisper of air between them.

"Mordred," she started to say, but he leaned down, hovering his lips above hers.

"Morgan, do you want this?" He asked as she felt the slight brush of his mouth against her. She could have said no, but that wasn't the truth. *Even with the wine, I know what I want.*

"Yes, I do," she replied, the last of the sound buried in his kiss. He held her hands tightly in his still, pressed against his chest.

"Tonight, be with me. Tomorrow, we'll return you to the castle, and you can fulfill your own destiny."

♛

DAWN HAD BARELY BROKEN over the sky before Mordred and Morgan were back on their horses, heading toward the fortress of Tintagel. She'd woken in his bed, but he wasn't in it, and she wondered briefly if he had regretted their night together. Morgan hurriedly dressed and found him in the Hall with the queen, making his farewells, wrapped in his cloak for travel. But seeing her enter, he hurried to Morgan's side and assured the queen of the Fae that they were off to destroy the Veil. Together.

"You're quiet this morning," he said, breaking the silence between them as they rode along the path.

"My head is a bit of a wreck, but otherwise, I am fine. This has all been much to take in." Morgan turned to give him a smile.

"I thought perhaps you were regretting last night."

"No, no regrets, Mordred. I am just worried about what is to come. With Igraine and with Merlin." He nodded at her words, and she smiled again, wanting him to know she did not regret their night together. *I know, though, that there will not be another. His world isn't mine.*

"Merlin will be opposed to our actions, you know this? He will be working to ensure the Veil survives. Can you stand against his wishes?" It was a fair question; she had been Merlin's daughter and apprentice. It stood to reason that there might be concern about her loyalty to the Fae's cause.

"I believe you that the magic of your people...our people...should not be used like this. Merlin's methods have not been just. He has used people, even killed people, to achieve his goal. Even if he means well with all this, I know that he is wrong for what he has done. I can oppose him. Have faith, Mordred." The castle silhouette peeked over the rise of the hill; they were nearly there.

"Oh, I have faith in you, Morgan. I believe you will set things right."

MORDRED LEFT her about a mile from the castle, turning his horse to head north. If Morgan needed him, he said, she had only to call for him, and he would come. She watched him ride away for a few moments before turning toward the castle farms that ringed the headland.

In the span of one night, she had changed her allegiance from Merlin's cause to Mordred and his kin. *Truth be told, Merlin has driven me from his path, by his actions to Igraine and me.* Morgan still felt that she bore the stain of the part she had played in all the deceit, but she hoped she could help to set things right now. With Uther's child in her belly, Igraine would be forced to make a choice, and that couldn't be helped. But what she chose to do, whether to listen to Merlin and give her baby to him for the prophecy, or live a life of her own making, that was on her. *Maybe, Morgan thought, she could help both her and the sidhe in the process.*

"Lady Morgan, good to see you are safe. With all the ruckus, people were starting to wonder what happened to you," one of the guards called to her as she neared the landbridge, an easy smile on his face. She'd seen him at his post for many years.

"I am well, thank you for kind words. But tell me what has happened?" He looked at her as if dumbstruck.

"You must have been away then, not to have heard. Prince Uther was slain, and Arthur Spear was taken as the culprit. Lord Ithyl even now takes the scoundrel to Uther's kingdom as payment for the crime." She didn't wait for another word from the soldier but gave her horse a soft kick to hurry forward. Mordred hadn't told her of Uther's death; perhaps he hadn't known. *I have to find Igraine.*

"Take care," Morgan shouted over her shoulder to the guard and cantered across the landbridge, heading for the turris. *What would Merlin say when he saw her, free from her crystal prison?* She had no idea.

♛

"Where is Lady Igraine?" Morgan called to Gisella, who was carrying a tray through the Great Hall.

"Mistress, she is not in her room. I am heading for the kitchens to see if she is with Edith."

"I'll check there, you keep searching for her. We must find her."

Morgan turned, heading back outside, toward the kitchens and that garden that Igraine loved so much. To her right, she heard a meow and saw Igraine's mouser sitting near the wall, looking at her expectantly.

"You are usually your mistress' shadow. Where is she off to?" He blinked in reply and curled up into a ball with his head tucked low. The heat from the sun-drenched stones must be warming his bones.

"Fine help you are," Morgan said, as she crossed the rutted path toward the kitchens. A gust of salty wind blew in her face and just caught the flicker of wings out of the corner of her eye. A sylph was hovering nearby.

"Cousin, I come to tell you your friend needs aid." The sylph's small face was blank of emotion,

"Igraine? Where is she?"

"The selkie bid me tell you, she keeps watch over her. She sits near the sea, along the old fisherman's path. After last night, the selkie fears she might do herself harm." The sylph flitted higher, the message now delivered.

"What happened last night?" Morgan whispered, trying not to attract the attention of the castle folk working around her.

"Why, she almost plunged into the sea. Some mortal stopped her. Ask her yourself." The air spirit lifted on the next breeze and was gone.

Morgan hurried away from the kitchens, turning instead toward the small path that led to the cliff. The wind was stronger now, away from the castle's thick walls, and she dearly wished that she had thought to bring something warmer than the thin cloak she wore. Looking down the narrow path, she saw a figure draped in green, sitting on a rock.

"Igraine?" Morgan yelled, but whether the figure heard her or not, she couldn't say. Careful not to trip along the rocky, slick way, she made her way closer, using the sharp edges of the wall for balance.

"Igraine?" Morgan called again, this time close enough that she knew the figure could hear her. At the water's edge, she saw a head poking out of the surf, watching them. The selkie was still here.

"Morgan," she said, in a flat and quiet tone. She didn't turn to look at the visitor.

"Oh, Igraine, I am glad I found you. I heard about Uther and Arthur. How can I help?" Morgan sat lightly on the edge of a stone next to Igraine, reaching out her hand to touch her shoulder. After a moment's hesitation, Morgan touched her gently, but she didn't move.

"It's too late for help now. Ithyl has taken him, and he'll be killed if he isn't already. I have been tricked and deceived, and now I face the future knowing Arthur died because of me." Her voice was muffled within the green cloak, but it barely sounded like her. This voice sounded defeated. Not the Igraine that Morgan had known these last few years.

"There must be something we can do to make things right. It might not be what you wanted, but you still have choices to make. Let me help you."

"Help? You want to help me? Where were you when this horrible deceit was played on me? Where were you when Uther was murdered and Arthur taken to be sacrificed? Where were you when any of us needed you?" She was raging now, screaming at Morgan as the wind blew down her hood. Her hair roiled around her, blowing into Morgan's face.

"Igraine, listen, I will admit to you that I could have done more, much more to protect you, but I did try to stop them from the deceit they played on you. I was imprisoned by Merlin for my defiance. I came back to try to make things right, to help." It wasn't a total lie, Morgan reasoned; she was trying to set things right, but not perhaps as Igraine might have thought. First and foremost, Morgan's mission was to keep Merlin's prophecy from coming true, damn the consequences. But she wouldn't hurt Igraine; Morgan would make sure not to take things that far.

She looked at Morgan, silent and staring, trying to decide if she could be trusted. Igraine had been hurt so much in the last day, Morgan couldn't imagine that she had any faith left in those around her. Igraine seemed about to turn from Morgan, shutting her out, and for a moment, Morgan thought about what spell she could cast to make the young woman trust her, but that felt like something Merlin would do. *No, she'll have to decide on her own.*

"What can we do?" she asked simply, looking at Morgan, with doubt and distrust.

"I know what Merlin wants, and we can make sure he doesn't get it. And maybe, I can call on some friends to help Arthur. But whatever happens, I will keep you safe. I promise." Morgan reached out to clasp Igraine's hand; it was so cold in Morgan's palm. *How long had she been sitting at the edge of the world, letting the wind freeze her?*

"Let's get you warmed up, and we can plan our next move," Morgan said, pulling her to her feet and leading her back along the path.

CHAPTER TWENTY-SEVEN

They crested the hill and turned toward the path leading back toward the kitchens. Igraine wanted to see Edith to try to soothe the poor woman if she could. Morgan could hardly deny her that, but she knew time wasn't on their side. *The longer we delay, the less likely Arthur can be saved. I need to call for Mordred's aid.*

"See to Edith, I will be with you shortly and then we must get you away from Tintagel. You can't stay here." They were sheltered against the side of the stables, out of sight from most everyone.

"Why can't I stay? I mean, I don't really want to stay, but am I in danger?" She sounded like the young girl that Morgan had first met years ago, naive and unaware of the world around her. Morgan knew Igraine couldn't picture how she might be in danger in her father's castle, even after all that had happened to her. *Still so naive, Morgan thought.*

"Igraine, Merlin never needed your magic to maintain the Veil, he needed your womb. He needed you to bear a child of Uther's, and that child would then be the security of the Veil. Merlin's plan is to take your baby, raise him to be a great leader, a king of all the realms. The prophecy then foretells that the king will fall to save his country. That is why we must get you away."

"And you knew of this plan? You knew all along?"

There was a split second when Morgan had to make a choice. She knew that choice would change whether Igraine trusted and listened to her, and ultimately, whether Igraine would escape.

"No, I didn't know. I learned only last night when I found out about Uther. I would never have gone along with the lie if I had known." Morgan said it, the lie leaving her mouth and never able to come back. Igraine visibly sighed in relief, but Morgan felt the weight of the words on her shoulders. *I know that weight will stay there. At least until I can make things right for her.*

"So now you know why we must get you away from here. If we can help Arthur, we will, but first, you must escape. Do you understand?" She nodded, but Morgan saw the questions lingering in her mind. She would want to know more and soon.

"Morgan, Igraine…" The voice startled them both, and they jumped at the sight of the battered Arthur Spear, dragging himself from the shelter of the cliff scrub brush. Morgan could see the remnants of magic on him, some spell that had helped to cloak him from sight. *The magic seems so familiar, almost a reflection of my own spells. Had Mordred done this?*

"Arthur!" Igraine stumbled forward and grabbed him, pulling him to them in the shelter of the stable wall. He had been beaten within an inch of living. Ithyl hadn't wanted any trouble on his trip north.

"How did you escape?" Morgan asked, rubbing her hands together, back and forth, and pulling the warmth and energy created between her palms as if it were sticky honey. The energy glowed a soft yellow, though she doubted the pair in front of her could see it. It was healing magic to help Arthur's wounds. She placed her palms against the nasty gash on his head, and he winced.

"A stranger, on the road. Dressed strangely. He freed me. Told me to run. Told me not to come back." He stuttered as he spoke, as if each word were a whip of pain to say. Morgan could see that the wound was starting to soften under the energy from her hand, the edges less angry and raw. He would need healing herbs and more effective skills than hers, but she was pleased to see him improving a little.

"Did he have red hair, and was he tall?" Igraine asked, and Morgan almost dropped her hands at the question. *Who is Igraine talking about?*

"Yes, how did you know? Did you send him?" Arthur asked, as puzzled as Morgan.

"No, well, yes, in a way. He saved me last night. I was thinking about...it doesn't matter...but he appeared and told me he would help you if...I didn't step from the cliff." Her words chilled Morgan. *Igraine had been thinking of ending her life?* She felt the weight of her lie, and all she had done settle even heavier on her back.

"I was so desperate that I agreed, and he disappeared. He must be some sorcerer, come to rescue us from Merlin's plan."

"What plan is that," Arthur asked, trying to sit up from Igraine's embrace. *He must be worried about being discovered, Morgan thought.*

"No time for that, you can tell him later. Time to leave. We'll need to get you from Tintagel before you are seen."

"The ship..."

"No, Arthur, the ship sailed. They are gone. We'll need another way," Igraine said, helping him to his feet. He leaned on her, letting the weight of his tall frame fall against her small shoulders.

"You'll need a walking stick, and traveler's garb, Arthur, and so you will Igraine, something to disguise you. And you'll need an escort to get out of Dumnonia. I need to call for help."

The sylph was back, flitting among the scrub bushes and stones, bouncing along on the currents of air. Morgan's companions couldn't see the air fairy, but Morgan didn't care about that now. There would be time for explanations later.

"I need you to take a message to Mordred of the *sídhe*. He must meet us to help Igraine escape. I won't be able to do this without his help. Tell him he must hurry." The sylph looked at her, cocking her head to the side as if considering Morgan's request. With a nod, she flashed away, heading east and out of sight.

"Who were you..."

"No time. We must hurry. Arthur, you must hide back in the bushes until we have the means to get you clear of the guards. Ithyl will be coming back to find you." Morgan tried to be gentle as she pulled him from Igraine's grasp, but he still gave a loud groan as she helped him find a spot out of sight.

"We must tell Edith," Igraine said, but Morgan cut her off with a raised hand.

"You can write to her after you are safe. Come with me and let's get you disguises and a wagon."

Morgan pulled the reluctant princess with her, as Igraine looked at the bushes hiding her love. With a tug, Morgan forced Igraine to follow as they rounded the edge of the stables.

"The laundry, we must go to the laundry and gather what we need. And we'll need food and herbs for Arthur. You go get clothing, and I'll get the rest. Be back here quickly." Igraine nodded and sprinted toward the laundry, the stone basin where the clothes were scrubbed on smooth stones and pinned to ropes to dry in the sea breeze. Morgan turned toward the turris and her rooms to get the herbs, hoping to avoid Merlin along the way.

♛

As quickly as her short legs would carry her, Morgan hurried to her chamber, keeping her gaze away from any who would stop her for chatting. Everyone was busy with their tasks or at least appearing busy as they gossiped about the events of the last few days, and that was just as well. The less prying eyes on what she was doing, the better.

She opened her chamber door to find Merlin sitting on a chair, drinking a mug of tea. She could smell the warm chamomile and honey. He seemed older, almost frail as he sat sipping his tea, watching her from under those bushy eyebrows.

"I see you escaped. I underestimated your powers," he said, but in a friendly, almost jovial voice. He almost looked proud.

"I escaped," she replied, without explanation. *He doesn't need to know about Mordred's help, unless he already knows, which is entirely possible.*

"I won't ask how you accomplished it. Some day perhaps you will tell me. For now, let us speak on the matter at hand. You are going to try to help our fair princess escape my evil clutches, no?" He took another sip of tea.

"My plans are my own. You made it clear that you have no wish for me in your life when you imprisoned me," Morgan said, shutting the door behind her and walking toward the brown satchel she had hanging from a peg in the wall.

"You misunderstood completely, Morgan. What I did was because I love you, and I couldn't hurt you in your foolish attempt to meddle in things beyond your reckoning. I have only ever wanted you in my life, from the moment of your birth to this very moment." He set down his cup and folded his long fingers in his lap.

"You mean the moment after I was born and my mother died? How did she die, Merlin? Couldn't a powerful sorcerer like you save her, or was her death part of some prophecy as well? Was she just another victim in your scheme to play deity?" Morgan took the satchel and began gathering herb jars and linen strips, roughly dumping them in as she hurried. *How long do I have before he tries to stop me?*

"Someone has been filling your head with nonsense, I see. That sounds like Eithne's words or one of her minions. So that is how you escaped the crystal chamber. Your mother's people came to the rescue and poisoned you against me."

"They told me the truth, and now, I am leaving to live among them. Away from you. Away from the lies and the treachery and the using of innocent people. I am done." Morgan had all the herbs she needed, and if she could get her spell book, she would have everything she needed from this room. It was next to Merlin on a small table.

"You think the *sidhe* are innocent? Who do you think killed your mother? It wasn't from bearing you, I can tell you that. She died because they wouldn't leave her alone, wouldn't leave her to live the life she had chosen for herself." He stood, picking up the book as he did so, holding it between his gnarled fingers.

"You lie, you've lied to all of us for years. Why should I believe you now?" Morgan took a step toward him.

"Don't believe me? Ask your new friends. Ask your kin how she died. A soldier of Eithne's killed her, striking her down with an iron blade. Ask them." He held the book out toward his daughter, offered on his palms. *Was this some kind of trick, Morgan wondered. Why would he give it to me?*

"Don't try to stop me from leaving," she said, as she quickly took the book from him. He held his empty palms toward her in supplication.

"I'll be waiting for your return," he said as Morgan hurried from the chamber.

♛

BACK AT THE STABLES, Igraine had arrived before Morgan, carrying an armload of cloaks and tunics. She must have seemed quite the sight to the women working the washing stones, but none would have asked her what she was about. Morgan had managed to grab some bread and cheese from the Hall on her way back. It would have to do.

"We must go," Morgan said, as Arthur pulled off his bloodstained tunic. His torso was littered with purple bruises, and Igraine gasped. There was a wagon near the stables that they could take, if they hurried.

Morgan heard the ruckus in the yard behind them, though they were out of sight. The sound of horses and men, the clank of armor as they climbed off their horses. Ithyl and his men were back.

"How will we get by them?" Igraine asked, easing the brown woolen tunic over Arthur's wounded left arm.

They waited in silence; Morgan had no answer for her, but she held her finger to her lips, sure that they needed to be quiet. Morgan needed time to think and time for Mordred to come. *He would have to come, or none of this would work.*

The sun was hot, intense on their backs, and she felt the thirst in her throat for the first time. It had been hours since Morgan had left the *sídhe* barrow, and she hadn't had a drop to drink in all that time. There was no telling how long they would have to wait for Ithyl's men to leave, but it must be coming near the midday meal. With any luck, they would all head for the Hall, and the trio could make their way to the wagon. Counting on luck seemed a poor prospect to Morgan.

She gazed up and noticed a cloud drifting across the sun, with others drawing closer. The light that had been roasting their backs was now filtered and darkening behind cloud after cloud. The breeze from the sea blew tendrils of fog around their feet, around the clumps of bushes and stable walls. After a few moments, Morgan could scarcely see Igraine and Arthur standing only feet from her.

"Hurry, to the cart, we can move under cover of fog," she whispered, and she felt the fog part in front of her as if it were waves sliced by the prow of a ship. This fog was magic, no fog gave way to human hands. It was *sidhe* magic. *Mordred, she thought.*

They made their way around the edge of the stone wall, into the white fog wall surrounding Ithyl's men. Morgan couldn't see them, but she could hear them; the horses were stomping their feet in fear, and men were calling down protections from their gods. She heard frightened men, but she didn't hear Ithyl's voice among them.

The women placed Arthur gently into the cart, along with their belongings, and Igraine and Morgan found the seat and the reins of the horse tethered to it. They slowly pulled the cart away from the stable, able to see a path of light straight in front of them, leading them toward the landbridge. Either side was a wall of mist as strong as any stone fortress.

At the bridge, Morgan tried to focus only on the light, not thinking of the land's edge on either side that could easily lead the wagon over into the sea below. The horse was sure-footed, and she had to trust that the creature knew the way. Morgan said a whispered prayer as they made it to the other side, where the hot sun was waiting. Over her shoulder, she saw the blanket of fog drape over the bridge, impenetrable.

"Crack the reins, Igraine. We must go." They had managed to make it out of the castle, but they were far from safe. *It won't be long before Ithyl comes looking for us, Morgan thought.*

CHAPTER TWENTY-EIGHT

1984

Arty felt Morgan's hand tug him through the portal, and his feet tripped on a stone as they stepped back through to their own time. He'd scrunched his eyes through the rush of air as they journeyed from there to here, from then to now. Opening them to the dimmer light of dusk, he saw Morgan's bent form in front of him.

"Are you alright?" Arty reached toward her, as she had let go of his hand. Her back was to him, but she looked smaller, almost stooped.

"Mum?" Lowen piped up, her carrot orange head popping out from behind a rock. "Mummy!"

Morgan sat on the edge of a crumbling wall and turned toward them for the first time. Her dark braid was now silvery white, hardly more than a few wisps of hair woven together. Her face looked desiccated and lined with soft furrows.

"She's old!" Lowen yelled at Arty as she ran out from her hiding place. "I knew she shouldn't have gone back!"

"Help me to the cottage, I'll be alright," Morgan said, lifting a hand toward Arty. Lowen shoved him out of the way and gave Morgan a hug, holding her in her small arms easily.

"We must call him, Mum. He can fix this," Lowen said, her face buried in the old woman's shoulder.

"No, that we won't do. Things will be fine, Lowen."

"But look at you, you need him. You need his magic."

"There is no need great enough to call your father, Lowen. Now, Arty, help me to the cottage. Then you go get some rest too, and we'll see you in the morning."

♛

ARTY WAS the last to join the other work-study students at the breakfast table the next day, where only a few limp pieces of bacon and some congealed scrambled eggs waited for him. He didn't have much of an appetite anyway, so he grabbed a piece of toast and poured a cup of coffee. He had hardly slept since making it back to his bed last night.

"You look a bit worse for wear, mate," Porsche remarked as he took a seat at the table. "Looks like you forgot to pack your hair dye; you've quite a bit of gray coming in." She smiled, but Arty found her comment rude. *Piss off, Porsche. At least I am not named after a car.*

"Ready for some real work today? No more orientation," Elsbeth said, peering over those owlish glasses of hers. She was reading a biography on Edward, the Black Prince. *Hadn't she been reading some Arthurian book yesterday? Talk about a bookhound, he thought.*

"Sure, I can't wait to dive into the work. It will be exciting to see what has already been found from Arthur's time." Arty bit into his toast. Cold as it was, it still tasted good to him with that thick layer of butter. Elsbeth stared at him.

"'Arthur?' Are you talking about the Victorian tourist period, as in Sir Arthur Conan Doyle? I don't think he ever traveled to Tintagel, at least as far as I know." Elsbeth closed the book and started gathering her things; it was almost time for the bus to arrive.

"No, I mean King Arthur. You know, the reason everyone comes to Tintagel?" Porsche and Elsbeth exchanged a look, and Elsbeth slung the bookbag over her shoulder.

"I have no idea who you are talking about. England never had a King Arthur."

♛

ARTY COULDN'T GET off the bus fast enough, sprinting away from the students shuffling back into the building to meet with Dr. O'Malley. *It will probably cost me my internship, but I have to get to Morgan and Lowen.*

He raced along the little path, turning the corner to see the cottage, still ablaze with all the flowers in their garden. Lowen and Morgan were sitting on the front porch, drinking tea.

"Something has happened," he said, banging their garden gate as he bustled through. Morgan looked even smaller in the bright light of day, wrapped in a knitted shawl.

"We know," Lowen said, sounding sullen. "You've screwed everything up. You couldn't just play your part, could you?"

"Enough, Lowen. It isn't Arty's fault. I knew the risk. I thought I could rewrite history and fix the mistakes I had made the first time, but we now see that I was wrong. Arty, sit, please." Morgan gestured for him to sit at her feet on the little porch, and he folded up next to her.

"When the past was new, when I lived through that time, with Igraine and Arthur Spear, it is true that I tried to thwart Merlin's prophecy. Mordred, Lowen's father, convinced me to help end the Veil to help his people - our people - and I agreed. To end Merlin's prophecy, Igraine's baby had to live, but he could not be the "Once and Future King." He could not fulfill his destiny as King Arthur. Back in the past, I had tried to help Igraine escape, but ultimately, I failed. It is why you know of King Arthur - because he was sacrificed just as the prophecy required.

"Someone has meddled with things in the past, causing that history to be changed. I need you to help set things right. I thought perhaps we could also save Arthur Spear in the process. I see now that if he lives, Merlin's prophecy won't come true, and that changes the future, changes that impact too many people. When Mordred wanted the Veil destroyed, I was willing to help because I didn't know the future. Now, I know what happens if there is no King Arthur, and that is not what is meant to be."

"Mum, you will wear yourself out. Rest now," Lowen said, reaching over a small hand to pat her mother's arm.

"We've made a mess of it, Arty. But we need to fix things, once and for all. We must ensure that Igraine's child serves his destiny. I've meddled enough to know that the end result is worse every time we try to change things. We need to set things right. One more journey back."

"But how and what would we do once we got there?"

"You and I will have to travel back and make sure that Arthur Spear does not change Igraine's destiny. I don't have the strength to do it alone. I'll need your help."

"You mean, kill Arthur Spear?"

"Whatever it takes to ensure Igraine's future is not altered. Remember, he was never supposed to live, Arty. A bitter pill to swallow, but it is the truth. I swore an oath centuries ago not to harm Igraine and her child, and I won't - but I made no such pledge to him."

Arty looked away from her wrinkled face and down at the trail of ants marching toward the garden from their nest. One after another, a neat line, doing their duty for the colony.

"I don't think I can," he said, without much sound to his voice. "Is it really so bad if King Arthur never becomes King Arthur?"

"Only if you want the world that you've known to exist again. Without Arthur, England isn't the same. If there's no King Arthur, it will change the course of everything." It was Lowen that piped up, sounding far older than her years.

"The choice is to change the fate of the world or change the fate of one man," Morgan said, stating it as simply as possible. Words that were that simple and that difficult. Arthur Spear and King Arthur could not exist together.

"I'll help you, but I can't promise when the time comes, that I can do what you ask of me. I really don't know if I can." *Can I leave*

Arthur Spear to his destined fate, to die for something he didn't do? Arty honestly didn't know.

"Lowen will come with us. Come back at sundown, I need to rest and prepare."

CHAPTER TWENTY-NINE

If Ithyl is north, we will head south, as far as the road will take us, Morgan thought. Perhaps they could find a ship for Arthur and Igraine to buy passage on, once they were free of the Veil. Morgan had the spell to make a path for them to leave - she just had to hope that her magic was strong enough to do it without Merlin.

On the rise of the small hill ahead of them, she saw a figure in scarlet, sitting on a beautiful gray horse. It was Mordred, waiting for them. Relief sighed from her; with his magic, she was sure that they would be able to get Igraine safely away. Merlin's words about her mother and her death were pricking the back of Morgan's mind, but there wasn't time for questions, not now. Once all this was over, and Igraine was safe, she'd ask Mordred to tell her everything. *It is just another of Merlin's lies. It has to be.*

"Who is that?" Igraine asked, still clutching the reins as they crested the hill. The horses, on their own accord, stopped in Mordred's path.

"A friend named Mordred. He helped us escape with that fog. We can trust him." He drew his horse alongside the wagon, only inches away from Morgan's side.

"I see you made it. I had no doubt, Morgan." He smiled warmly and looked at Igraine, waiting to be introduced.

"Mordred, this is Princess Igraine. That is Arthur Spear resting in the back."

"Thank you for your help, we couldn't have made our way without your fog. It covered our escape."

"I am glad to have been of service. Morgan is a new friend but a dear one."

Morgan glanced over her shoulder, fearing that Ithyl could be upon them if they lingered on the road. "Perhaps we should move along," she said.

"Yes, I suppose we should. I will ride alongside you for a bit until I know you are safely away."

Igraine gave the reins a tug, and the cart lurched forward, with Mordred riding at their side.

♛

THEY HAD BEEN RIDING for some time, though truth be told she didn't know how long. Her mind was distracted by thoughts of her mother, Merlin, and Ithyl. *Why hadn't Ithyl been with his men in the yard at Tintagel? Perhaps, he had gone on north with only Uther's body. Maybe he had been in the turris with the king discussing what to do next.* It was nothing, she told herself, even though her belly told her otherwise. Igraine's cry woke her from her daydreams.

"Morgan, it is Ithyl. Look!"

Igraine's uncle sat on his warhorse, blocking the road with several soldiers at his flanks. They had no weapons drawn; they only blocked the path.

"We were wondering how much longer you would be," he said, giving his horse a slight tap to the side to move it forward.

"Uncle, why are you here?" Igraine replied, and Morgan heard Arthur groan from behind them.

"My dear niece, I couldn't let you go just yet. We need to discuss this with your father before you can head off to Gaul or Byzantium or wherever else you think you are heading. Come, let us turn back toward Tintagel and meet him along the road. He should be here shortly. I sent a rider for him."

Igraine turned to look at Morgan, and she, in turn, looked to Mordred.

"We should listen to what he has to say. There is time enough for fighting if it comes to that." Mordred said, reading Morgan's thoughts.

It took some doing, but they managed to turn the cart around and retrace their tracks back toward the castle. Morgan heard Igraine crying softly next to her, and she knew what was troubling her. *Every step closer to Tintagel, the less likely she and Arthur would escape this mess.*

Morgan saw the king's party ahead of them, a small group easy to spot with the king's charger decked out in royal livery. King Geraint had only four guards with him, less than the men who followed Ithyl. The king's brother rode ahead of the wagon, halting to greet them. There were no dwellings or farms on this stretch of the road; they were all alone.

"Brother, thank you for coming. I appreciate the speed of your haste. We haven't much time," Ithyl said, as Igraine pulled the cart to a halt.

"Ithyl, what is the meaning of this? You summon me to meet you on the road, like a common page? And why is Igraine on that cart? What is going on?" It seemed the king's eyes were yet good enough to spot his daughter at a distance, even wearing her homespun cloak. *Perhaps it was her russet hair that gave her away, Morgan thought.*

"Apologies for rousing you from your rest, Brother. You see, this conversation is best held away from the turris, away from the courtiers' listening ears and spying eyes. Bear with me, and I will explain all, Geraint." Out of the corner of Morgan's eye, she saw Mordred pull his horse slightly away from them. Igraine nudged Morgan's knee; she had seen this as well.

"Your decisions have endangered Dumnonia. It is no secret that I disapprove of this scheme of yours, with the Veil conjured by your pet sorcerer. I've tried to do things your way, to put my faith in the magic he claims will protect us, but after the murder in the village, I knew I had to act." The king opened his mouth to speak, but Ithyl raised his hand to silence him. Igraine took a sharp breath.

"Whether the breach was real or a trick by your sorcerer to convince Igraine to wed Uther, I don't know, and I don't care. You either killed your own people or left them vulnerable to those Wessex wolves. I cannot let this pass."

"Ithyl, you speak treason. I could have you in irons for this." Geraint bellowed at his brother, pulling himself up to his full height in the saddle. Even old, the king looked daunting on his warhorse.

"Brother, you have a choice. We can either battle for the throne, and you will lose, costing many lives of good men, or you can step down and live in peace in exile. The choice is yours, but you should think carefully about your answer." Ithyl sounded utterly relaxed as if they were discussing the casking of ales. *How could he speak of removing the rightful king with such ease? Betrayal at the hands of a brother,* Morgan thought.

"You should know me well enough, Ithyl, to know I would never step down. I would never leave Dumnonia to a man who would remove his own brother and king." The soldiers near their monarch were on edge, hands poised on the hilts of their swords. Ithyl's men matched their movements; any moment, a fight would break.

"Perhaps this will help you reconsider, Geraint. I will allow Igraine and her wounded love to leave, unharmed, if you, and the fair princess, renounce your claims to the throne. If not..." He didn't finish the sentence, but instead, pulled his horse close to Igraine's side of the wagon.

"My Lords, I fear things may come to blows if we do not calm ourselves," Mordred interjected, speaking for the first time. Both men looked at him in surprise.

"What business is this of yours, stranger?" Geraint asked.

"As friend and kin to the Lady Morgan, I wish to spare us all violence. Perhaps I can be of assistance. Forgive me if I am speaking out of turn, but it appears that Lord Ithyl has every intention to fight, here and now, on the road. Why else lure the king from his fortress?" Mordred looked at Ithyl, who nodded twice.

"And King Geraint, you are outmatched and will surely lose any fight today. But what if there were a third way? What if the Lady Igraine and her injured friend were my guests while this negotiation commences? Lady Morgan can return to Tintagel to guarantee that I will keep them both safe but secure with me. Once the details are determined, I will release my guests to their fortunes."

"And why would I agree to this, stranger, when as you say, I have a clear advantage now?" Ithyl asked, a smirk on his face.

"Because your people will never accept your rule if you ambush the rightful king to steal the throne. However, they will accept a transfer of power that is done in a calm and reasoned way." Mordred spoke smoothly, and Ithyl's smirk faded to a grimace.

"And you propose to take my daughter as a hostage?" King Geraint's hands were clutching his reins, knuckles white.

"An honored guest, My Lord. Lady Morgan has been to my kin's hall; she can attest that it befits a princess." For the first time, these men expected Morgan to speak. Igraine looked at her, fear clearly on her face.

"I trust Mordred, he will keep Igraine safe. It avoids bloodshed this day. We should listen to him." Geraint looked at Morgan, taking a pause to weigh her words. She couldn't see a good way out of the situation; she and Mordred could cast magic but likely not before someone was injured. Ithyl was close enough to Igraine to find a dagger into her side. Morgan was not the master of immobilizing spells like Merlin.

"So be it. Stranger, you have the care of my daughter. Do not fail your duty. Ithyl, you and I will return to Tintagel and discuss your proposal. Perhaps we can find a way through this." Morgan knew the wily king was already thinking about how Merlin could help him; it was plain on his face.

"Agreed, Brother. Just so there is no secret between us - you have your sorcerer, but I have my own. Have no illusions that Merlin will intercede on your behalf against me. We decide this as men, not those who cower behind magic." Ithyl signaled his guards, and they fell into line behind the king's party.

"I'm frightened, Morgan," Igraine said, as Mordred pulled back close to our cart. Arthur, who had been silent behind them, was not awake to hear her.

"Mordred will take care of you. You have my word. He can be trusted."

"Lady Morgan, join me on my horse, will you?" Ithyl called to Morgan, and she slipped from the cart as Mordred nodded at her. Igraine and Arthur were now in the care of the Fae.

CHAPTER THIRTY

"Shall we be off, then?" Mordred asked, and Igraine wasn't sure they had a choice. Arthur was too wounded to fight, and they had nowhere to run to. *What choice do we have?*

"Before we go, I would ask you, why are you doing this?" Igraine had heard Morgan's words that this man could be trusted, but why would he involve himself in this affair? *Was it purely out of kindness?*

"You seem to doubt my motives, Lady Igraine. Why would I wish to involve myself in the affairs of men? Because the affairs of men involve me and my kind, whether we like it or not. Your father's blessing for the magic that created the Veil caused harm to my people, the *sídhe*. We have a stake in this world as well." His horse stomped at the dirt trail, ready to be on its way. By the way he shifted in his saddle, Igraine could tell he was too.

"Are you the sorcerer who is helping Uncle Ithyl?" She felt a knot in her stomach growing larger with his every word.

"You are perceptive, Princess. I thought Ithyl and I had gone to great pains to keep that a secret. What Ithyl does not know is I have my own reasons for helping him. For now, that includes hosting you and your injured friend. Come. I'll even have someone tend to his wounds.

That should please you." He tugged his reins, and the horse cantered away.

"We have no choice, Arthur, not yet. But once you are better, things will be different." Igraine heard him groan a little at the mention of his name. *Thank the goddess; he is still alive. I'll accept Fae healing if it saves him.* Igraine gave the reins a flick, and the horse trailed behind the retreating figure ahead of them.

♛

THEY RODE ON, past the path back to Tintagel, heading along a lonesome cow path that jostled the wagon. She could hear Arthur's groans at each bump and rut.

"Igraine, where are we going?" He was struggling to sit up against the wagon wall.

"We are going with Mordred, a friend of Morgan's. He is watching over us while...things are decided." He didn't need to know they had no choice in the matter, she reasoned. *Why worry him when we are helpless to change things.*

"You should go," Arthur said. "Leave me and escape. I'll be alright." Igraine saw their guide slowing near a small hill with a stone entrance.

"Nonsense. Edith would thrash me senseless. Now, hush and rest." She smiled over her shoulder, hoping to brighten his mood. He didn't return the smile.

"I am serious. Get away. We know nothing of this person's motives."

Igraine had the same suspicions, but there wasn't anything to say, nor could she when their host was now within earshot.

"Let's get you mended," she said, hoping he knew what she would have said after that. *Then we can run.* He nodded but said nothing.

"We are here, friends. Unfortunately, only the *sídhe* or those of *sídhe* blood can enter our barrow. However, I promised you shelter and care, and you shall receive it. My brethren will prepare temporary lodgings." He slipped from his saddle and stepped toward the dark passageway. He was gone only a few moments when he returned with a trail of figures behind him.

"Althae will tend to your wounds, she is a great healer," Mordred said, gesturing to a woman to approach the wagon. She carried no salves or bandages with her, nothing but a gentle smile on her face.

"Peace, friend. Mordred bids me help you mend. Close your eyes and let me attend to you."

Igraine watched, hawklike, to see what this stranger would do. *After all, what was stopping this Mordred from slitting our throats? We don't know him at all, Igraine thought; she had only Morgan's word that he would help them. Perhaps he had deceived Morgan as the enchantment on Uther had deceived her.* She shook her head to chase away the thought, and Arthur looked at her in confusion. They hadn't had a chance to talk since everything had happened.

"Close your eyes, young man. I need you to focus on your wounds and not your pretty companion. She'll be there when you open them again." The Fae woman chuckled and climbed quickly into the wagon, kneeling before Arthur. She rubbed her hands together fiercely before extending them over Arthur's torso. He closed his eyes.

Igraine wanted to watch, but her curiosity at the actions around her drew her focus. A large tent of heavy fabric now stood off to the side of the barrow. She could see within the open flap a chair and a rug over the mossy ground. A platter of food rested on a small table, and a pitcher of what she hoped was fresh water.

"Come, Igraine, refresh yourself. Althae will bring Arthur to you when she is finished." Mordred said, offering her a hand down from the cart. She clasped it and noticed for the first time that his skin had a sheen like pearls.

"We are grateful for your hospitality, Sir. Thank you for all you do to help Arthur. He has been treated cruelly by my uncle." She released his hand as soon as her foot touched the earth, and he led her toward the tent.

"The Fae are renowned for their hospitality, among other things. I would dishonor my kin to do otherwise. Besides, you are friends of Morgan, and she is special to us. Her mother was a close companion of our queen." He raised the tent flap, and Igraine stepped inside a cozy and comforting space, away from the wind and sun from outside. A goblet of water waited for her on the table. *Would it be safe to drink it, she wondered, knowing the legends of the Fae.*

"Fear not, Princess. You need no food tester with me," Mordred chuckled, gesturing toward the goblet, and she picked it up to gulp.

"Thank you," Igraine said, after a deep drink. The water was cold and delicious. She took a seat by the table and plucked an apple from the basket.

"Princess, I am not one for games. I'd prefer to deal honestly with you. Your uncle will not rest until he has the throne. Your father will have to relinquish it, or he will die, it is as simple as that." Mordred took the other seat, picking up an apple of his own. He passed the red orb back and forth in his hands slowly.

"My father won't easily agree to it if that is what Ithyl thinks. Even to save me." She took a bite of her apple, and the sharp sweetness filled her mouth. It was the best apple she had ever tasted.

"Whether the King of Dumnonia is your uncle or your father is immaterial to me. The only thing the Fae care about is ending the Veil. Ithyl intends to do just that. Your father's cruel deceit on you cannot be undone, but you can still live the life you dream of, with your love." He paused and took a bite of his apple, slowly piercing the flesh with his white teeth.

"I just want to be away, with Arthur, from this place, and forget about magic and duty and trickery. Of course, I do not wish any harm to my father, but this is no longer my home."

"That is understandable, certainly. Perhaps we can help each other. You wish to go live your life, I wish to ensure that no mortal raises another Veil to harm my people. We can accomplish our goals together." He took another bite of the apple, and a drop of juice dropped on the smooth oak table.

"How?"

"The child, in your womb. Let us care for you until it is born. Then you and Arthur may leave, and we will tend to the child. The babe will ensure no Veil can be raised again." He stared at her over the top of the apple, his eyes boring into her.

"You want me to give you the baby?" Igraine didn't know what to say to that. She hadn't had one peaceful moment to consider what would happen to the baby in her belly, but giving it to anyone had never entered her mind. And yet, perhaps it should have. *Was raising a child something I want? Could I even do it if I leave Tintagel?*

Mordred seemed to be reading her thoughts. "We would raise the child as our own, care for it and see to its every need. Uther's bloodline comes from the Fae, and so the child would be kin of ours and dear to us. The child would never want, Igraine. And you could be free." He set the apple on the table, pausing to dab at his lips with a small linen cloth before rising from his seat.

"Think on it. Speak with Arthur and make plans for your future. I believe Althae brings him to you now." The tent's flap opened just then, and Arthur walked unassisted, looking whole if still battered.

"I will come back to check on you both shortly. In the meanwhile, know that my kin watches over you so no harm shall come. We ask that you do not wander from this haven, though. Please stay and rest." With a small bow, he left the tent, passing by Arthur as he did so.

"Are you better, Arthur?" Igraine asked as he stepped toward the chair. She pushed the platter of bread and cheese toward him.

"Yes, I am. I still ache and feel weak, but that healer has done a miracle." He sat heavily in the chair, and she saw that lopsided smile that she loved creep back onto his face. "What were you talking about?"

She didn't know where to start. There was so much she needed to tell him. So much had happened and it had changed her life forever. He had no idea. All he knew was Uther was dead.

"Eat, drink, and then I'll tell you everything. There is much to tell and much to decide."

CHAPTER THIRTY-ONE

Ithyl's men kept watch over the king as they returned to the castle. Morgan wondered if perhaps Geraint would try to rally his men to him, but it was clear that Ithyl's men had been busy in their absence. Ithyl's standard greeted them as they crossed the landbridge. There was fresh blood on the grass.

"You see, Geraint, I have the superior forces. Those of your men who did not surrender were put to the blade. You have no hope for reinforcements. Even as we speak, Uther's body makes its way to his father with the word that I am in command, that I slew his killer, that I am now king."

At the door to the turris, Morgan saw Merlin standing, leaning on a walking stick.

"And what did your sorcerer do to assist you, to defend your castle? Nothing." Ithyl said, pulling his horse to a stop. She slid from the saddle, jumping to the ground.

"Morgan, are you well," Merlin asked, and she nodded.

"Come, let's finish this, Geraint. I have the papers prepared for you to sign. Abdicate, and I will give you passage to Gaul. You can take Igraine with you."

The king was slower to come down from his horse, but he found his feet on the ground and walked toward Merlin. "Come now, Ithyl, you'll never let me leave these lands alive. You know that." Without waiting for a reply, he walked into the Hall with Merlin shuffling behind him. The rest of their party followed in his wake.

"Don't be a fool, Geraint. I said I would let you leave, and I will. I wish no bloodshed. Just sign the damn paper, and you can be away with your daughter."

The king did not head for his throne, but instead, he took a seat at one of the tables, sitting heavily on the bench. For the first time, he removed his gloves and helm.

"I think not, Brother. I will not flee my people. Kill me if you must, but I am not going anywhere." He looked up at Ithyl, glowering above him, but Morgan saw no fear in his face. Merlin stood at his shoulder. *Does he think his sorcerer can save him?*

"Then if you will not leave, I will have no choice but to kill you and Igraine. The people will have to accept their new king." Ithyl made no move upon the pair.

"There is another way, My Lord," Merlin said, breaking the stalemate. "What if the king recognizes you as his heir, you and your progeny. No need for bloodshed at all. Lady Igraine has no wish to rule, I am sure she would agree to it."

"You should ask Igraine that question," Morgan said, blurting out her words without thinking. The men turned to look at her for the first time, surprised at her presence.

"You are all so quick to decide her fate, and yet you never ask what she wants. Igraine is Princess of Tintagel; do not be so quick to cast her aside."

"What Igraine wants is not a concern to me. She can live if she abdicates her rights. If she does not, well, then she will fall to my sword. I know she will make the right choice, she is no fool."

Morgan was angry, as angry as she could remember. These old men deciding the fates of others as easily as discussing the weather. She wondered if her own magic could stop Ithyl. Could she summon a spell that would bind him and allow the king's remaining men to capture him? *Perhaps she could stop his heart beating in his chest, grip it with an invisible hand and squeeze the life from him. She had never tried dark magic before; there had never been a need, but perhaps it could be their salvation.* Surely, once Ithyl took the throne, she thought, he would be certain Merlin and Morgan were out of his way. *Why wasn't Merlin doing something?*

"Enough," the king said. "Allow me to think on this. Can you at least give me that, Brother?"

"You have until sunrise, Geraint. I wait no longer than that. Sorcerer, start whatever befouled work you do to draw down the Veil. Whatever else happens, that comes down." Ithyl stormed from the table, flanked by his loyal soldiers, leaving the king, Merlin, and Morgan alone.

"What can you do to thwart him, Merlin? He claims a sorcerer protects him, keeps guard over him."

"There is something binding me, My Lord. I have felt myself weakening over the last few days. It cannot contain my powers fully, but I am diminished. Even with Morgan's help, I might not be able to stop whoever guards Ithyl. Yet…" Merlin stopped, pausing to sit on the bench near the king.

"What is it?" Morgan asked, wondering what idea could be rattling around in that crafty brain of his.

"We might be able to counter the magic if we knew who was behind it all and cast it back against them. A reflection spell might do the trick, but we'd need help," Merlin said, speaking to his daughter.

"You have until dawn. After that, I have to decide if the kingdom's needs outweigh the life of my daughter."

"MERLIN, what did you mean? Who would help us?" He was rooting around in his study, flinging parchment about as he stooped over the old chest.

"It has been so many years. I don't know if she would help, but we must try." He pulled a rolled scroll from the trunk, tied with a leather strap.

"Who? What are you saying? We don't even know for sure who is helping Ithyl." Morgan sat heavily in the chair nearest him, suddenly exhausted by it all.

"Hmmm? Oh, I have a good idea who has stirred this pot. But let's first see if she will aid us. Without her, all is lost." He shook the parchment at her and smiled before reaching for his cloak on the wall.

"Come, we must hurry. We must ride to Nectan's Kieve as quickly as we can."

"The gorge where that old hermit used to live? Why there?" Morgan followed the old man as he dragged his leg toward the chamber door before grabbing his walking stick.

"To see her, of course. To see Nimue. She lives at the edge of the water at the bottom of the gorge. We must see your mother's sister. There is no time to lose."

CHAPTER THIRTY-TWO

My aunt. Aisling's sister. Never in all the years with Merlin had he said that Morgan's mother had a sister, and she lived only a few miles from Tintagel. Nimue, he had called her.

"Why didn't you tell me about her?" They were on horseback and heading toward the Kieve, down a narrow, switchback path.

"What is there to tell? Your mother's kin did not take kindly to her leaving the Fae world to bear a human child. We had no dealings with them."

That is it. That is all the explanation I am going to get. They rode on, each in their own thoughts and letting the woods' silence drape over them. Morgan was so tired of secrets, of not knowing even basic things about her own life. *If I ever have a daughter, I will never keep secrets from her.*

"We must continue on foot," Merlin said, halting his horse at the bottom of the gorge, its walls steep and slick with the mists from the waterfall that plunged from above. She slid from her saddle and followed him as he limped toward a pool of water in the distance.

Birds were calling, their song breaking the forest quiet, along with the sound of Merlin's shuffling feet. The grotto held shadows, and

Morgan squinted to look for signs of a house where someone might be hiding away from the world. She saw nothing but craggy stones.

"Nimue, we are in need. Please come meet with us," Merlin called, his voice echoing around us. The birds cawed in reply.

"Is she here?" Morgan asked, still scanning for any signs of a dwelling or even a cave.

"Yes, she's here. I can feel her magic. Can't you? You should be able to tell." He was chiding her, even now, lecturing on her skills. *I am ever the apprentice, it seems.*

She saw a flash of white before she heard a sound. She turned to see a woman wearing a long white gown, walking through the woods toward them.

"What brings you to my haven, Merlin? It has been more years than I care to remember." Like Morgan, she had dark hair, but unlike her, she was tall and graceful, lithe in her snowy gown.

"Nimue, we need your help. The King of Dumnonia will fall if we do not assist him. Fae magic works against him. It also hinders me, draining the life and energy from me. Please. I fear for us all." Merlin never said please, not that Morgan could recall. She watched as the woman looked him over, examining his face and frame — her aunt, unknown to her.

"And this must be Aisling's child. I see your Fae spirit, though you do not yet know your full worth. A pity."

"I didn't know my mother had a sister," Morgan replied, for lack of something to say. "Merlin never told me."

The woman chuckled lightly, and her smile reminded Morgan of Mordred's. "No, I suspect he would not have. Not after everything. All that is in the past, though. I hold no grudge; Aisling made her choice freely. Not wisely, but freely. Her fate was her own. As is the fate of this king you speak of. I will not meddle in the affairs of men." She turned as if to leave them on the bank of the pool, back into the shadows and forest.

"Nimue. He is killing me, as surely as he killed Aisling. You must help me for her sake."

Morgan stared at her father, her mouth open wide in shock. *Killing him? Who was killing him?*

"You know this? Are you certain?" Nimue turned back to look at the crumpled figure clutching his walking stick.

"Look for yourself and see the truth," he said. "As you knew the truth about Aisling and were exiled for it."

Nimue said nothing but walked toward the pool near his feet. She bent down, drawing a small silver cup from a white silken bag hanging from a belt at her waist. She drew the cup along the surface of the water, standing up when the cup was full. She held the cup in both hands, staring at the surface as the birdsong filled the quiet. After several moments, she drew the cup to her lips and drank the water, closing her eyes tightly.

"You speak true, Merlin. Mordred has cursed you. He will drain your life unless he is stopped. He plots with the usurper, but his aim is more than securing the throne. I cannot see more than that." She placed the cup back into the small purse.

"Mordred? Are you certain? But I know him. He wouldn't do this." Morgan said, stepping closer to both Merlin and Nimue. Her head was reeling. *Mordred is behind this? How could it be?*

"Child, Mordred is not as he seems. He killed my sister, disguised by magic, so that none of the Fae would know he had struck the blow. None save me and my visions. The queen did not believe me and banished me for treachery against her own blood. Mordred is powerful and clever; believe him at your peril. It cost Aisling her life. Merlin, I will help you in debt to Aisling's memory. What do you need of me?"

"I brought a reflecting spell, an old and powerful one, with the hope that you would help us cast it. It would turn Mordred's magic against him and draw down the defenses against the usurper, Ithyl. Once defenseless, my magic can thwart him and keep the rightful king on the throne. Then, I can deal with Mordred. As I should have years ago."

Nimue turned from us, heading away from the water's edge. "Follow me, and we shall see if your spell can confound a prince of the *sidhe*."

"And your father agreed to…do that to you?" Arthur asked after Igraine had told him everything that happened at Tintagel.

"He knew, Merlin knew, only Uther and Morgan were unaware of the treachery. When she learned, she tried to stop them, and Merlin locked her up. That is how she met Mordred; he rescued her."

Arthur's blue eyes were staring at Igraine's chin, not looking into her eyes. He was angry, that was easy to see, but she feared he might turn that anger on her, blaming her that she should have known, should have been able to tell that Uther wasn't really Arthur when they had shared her bed.

"I'll kill them," he said simply. "Merlin and your father."

"You may get your wish if Ithyl has anything to say about it. As for Merlin, I don't care what happens to him, but my father…" Igraine stopped. *How can I say that I both love and hate the only parent I have left in the world? What he did was monstrous, but can I wish him dead?*

"We'll leave. We'll run and find our way to Gaul. We'll catch up with *The Gloria* and make for Carthage. Damn both of them." For the first time since Igraine had told him about Uther, he looked into her eyes. She saw nothing but protection and love there.

"And the baby?" They couldn't pretend it wasn't at the heart of everything that they would now ever be.

"The three of us. We'll leave and never look back." He stood up, stretching after sitting for so long. He came to her, lifting her chin with his long, tender fingers, so rough on her skin. Bending low, he kissed her, with a gentle intensity, before breaking away.

"Let's go. Now."

"We can't. Mordred said to stay here, to wait for word." Arthur spread a linen cloth on the table. He piled the apples, bread, and cheese into the center, tying it into a makeshift satchel and stuffed it into a bag of supplies from the cart.

"I'm not waiting for his blessing. That man wants something and we won't wait to find out." Igraine hadn't told him what Mordred had said about the baby while Arthur was being healed.

"He wants the baby to raise as a Fae child. He promised to guard the child." Arthur stopped for a moment, hand still clutching the bag.

"What did you tell him?"

"Nothing. I agreed to nothing."

"Good, because this child is not to be bartered with or used as some prize. Not by your father and not by this Fae Lord." His words flowed over her like a balm, soothing her in a way that she had desperately needed since the nightmare began. She had never considered abandoning the baby, but knowing that Arthur's love and care would be for them both - it was all she needed to hear.

"Let's go," Igraine said, reaching out her hand to squeeze his.

THE AFTERNOON SUN was low in the sky. It would be dark soon, and Igraine wondered if perhaps they should steal away in the night, but Arthur wanted to get as far away as quickly as they could. The cart was gone, as were the horses. There wasn't a trace of activity near their tent - no scouts or guards that they could see.

"What now?" Igraine asked, following Arthur away from the barrow.

"We walk on shank's mare, our own feet carrying us as far as we can get in the light. We'll head south, and at the first village we find, we'll send word to Morgan. We'll need her to pierce the Veil so we can leave the kingdom." He pulled Igraine's hand, helping her climb over the stony hills that formed a ring around the barrow.

"Arthur, I'm afraid." *How could they hope to make it to Gaul with no money, no horses, no protection from Ithyl or Igraine's father, let alone the Fae? It was impossible.*

"Have faith, Lady. You keep worrying, and you'll end up with wrinkles like my ma." He looked back to give her his crooked grin.

"I'll tell her you said that," Igraine replied, but he shook his head.

"No, you'll *write* to her that I said that and someone will read it to her. We won't be back to Tintagel, ever again." He squeezed her hand, and she pushed the doubts as far from her mind as she could. *We have to make it.*

♛

They'd been walking a while, pausing briefly to drink from a brook that ran near the path. Moonrise couldn't be long now. Igraine didn't know which direction they were heading, but Arthur seemed to know. *It must be his sailor's keen sense of direction, she thought.*

"Let's find a hollow and rest until dawn," he said, finally letting go of her hand. Her fingers were cramped and tingling, but she didn't care.

She felt the wind swirling the edge of her cloak, even though the air was still. A strange scent washed over her, like ripe raspberries, but nothing grew near them beyond moss and grass clumps. Before she could turn to ask Arthur, she saw the flash of scarlet. Mordred stood before them.

"Now Princess, I thought I had advised you to stay at the barrow? The road is not safe," he said, smiling. Arthur stepped between them.

"Sir, we thank you for all you have done, but we are leaving. Please let us go on peace." Arthur spoke as he shielded her with his tall body. His neck was tanned like a horse's saddle from the sun, sprinkled with bright freckles and an old scar. *She'd have to ask him about that scar later.*

"I had hoped to keep things congenial, but I must insist. The lady comes with me. You were only a courtesy, but if you wish to leave, be my guest." Mordred signaled toward the roadside.

"I will not abandon her or her child. You shall have neither." Igraine saw Mordred smile again, teeth white and sharp.

"Enough, boy. This ends. I have little patience for games. Step aside, or you die." Mordred drew his hands up to his chest, arms stiff and open as if he were about to embrace someone. Igraine saw a greenish glow pulsing in his palms, the color of fresh May grass.

"Morgan won't take kindly to this, your betrayal of her friends."

She took a small step to the side so she could see him in full as she spoke. *If I can reason with him, maybe he will stop his plan to hurt us.*

"Morgan will do and think as she is told. Do not expect her to save you from what I have planned. I have worked too hard to be thwarted by some silly half-Fae girl." The green light coursed from his palms, creeping along his fingers until his hands glowed from it. His smile was now a smirk.

"I nearly died once already, I suppose I can take another crack at it, Elfling." Arthur crossed his arms in front of his chest.

"Insults to the end. So be it then," Mordred said, flexing his hands. The green light poured from him, spilling out into the air that separated them from him. In a moment, it struck Arthur square in his chest, weaving under his folded arms. Igraine heard him cry out, the sound loud in her ear.

"You mortals never learn to leave things to your betters. Meddlesome creatures, the lot of you." Arthur dropped to one knee, his arms now reaching out in a perverse mirror of Mordred's own.

"Run," Arthur grunted, still held by the green light. Before Igraine could tell him no, the next scream of pain came from the Fae Lord himself.

The light was gone, soaking into the ground at Arthur's feet. Instead, Igraine saw Mordred doubled over, his hands balled into fists of pain.

"No," he bellowed. "How..."

She pulled Arthur's arm as hard as she could, dragging him from the ground as they ran, scrambling up the bank to the road. It was almost dark, and the moon was clouded over. There before them were three dim figures - an old woman, a tall man, and a child.

"Hurry," Igraine said, still tugging Arthur, pulling him toward the group. She didn't care who they were; freedom was down that road.

"Igraine," the man said, and she stopped. That voice, she knew it. It was the sorcerer from the night on the cliff. *Maybe he can save us.*

"Igraine, please listen to me. You must come back to Tintagel, to Merlin and your father. The future must not be changed."

"Stranger, we are running, and you should too. The Fae Lord, Mordred, is at heel."

The child tugged at the old woman's arm and whispered, "He's here, I want to see him."

From behind her, Igraine heard a sound, and without looking, she knew Mordred was climbing the hillside. Their only escape would be this strange sorcerer.

"Help us, please," Igraine said, hurrying to gather near them. The old woman kept her hood drawn around her, but Igraine caught a quick glimpse of her craggy face. *Have we met before at the castle? She seems familiar to me.*

"I don't know how you managed that, but Merlin's reflection spell cannot stop me," Mordred yelled, cresting the rise. He was moving slowly as if something was dragging behind him. He stopped when he saw the others near Igraine.

"Strike him," Igraine hissed, waiting for the sorcerer to move.

"We've come to escort Igraine back to Tintagel. Leave her alone." The young man's voice wavered; he sounded as fearful as Igraine felt. His hands were in the pockets of that strange coat he wore, not ready to cast a spell.

"You should have brought help then," Mordred said, taking a few slow steps toward them.

"He did," the old woman said, still keeping her face from Igraine. "I don't want to hurt you, Mordred, even after all you've done, but I will if I must." Her withered hands were now raised before her, glowing pale white in the dim moonlight.

"I didn't expect this, I must say, though I suppose I should have. We made a bargain, do you remember?" The green glow crept again into his palms, albeit paler and slower than before.

"I do. I remember everything. But you lied to me when I made that pledge. You lied about your real purpose, lied about what happened to my mother, lied to trick me into helping you. Everything you did and said was a lie. It ends now as does my pledge to you." The white light flashed and sparked, pulsing strongly from her hands and pooling near her feet. She was almost as short as the child hovering by her side.

"Do you think your magic can best me? Remember who I am and remember what you are!"

"You may be surprised at what I've mastered over the years." And with that, she sent the light from her. It cascaded out and struck him, the light piercing his side as he tried to shield himself, to dodge the blow. Igraine saw dark crimson drops flow to the ground from his scarlet tunic.

"Take Igraine," the old woman said, speaking to the child. The girl stared at the crumpling figure but did not move. "Now, Lowen!" She barked at the girl, who jolted and tugged at Igraine's sleeve. She grabbed Arthur to pull him with her, but the girl shook her head.

"Not him, just you."

"Then I am not going," Igraine said, still pulling on Arthur.

"Arty, help me," the girl whined, and the tall sorcerer stepped toward them.

Before Igraine could see what he planned for them, green light crackled and sparked, striking at the old woman. The white light flickered but did not falter.

"Hurry," the old crone said as she sent another wave against Mordred.

"Igraine, run. I'll catch up." Arthur said, releasing her hand. Igraine reached back for him, but the tall man pulled her away, snatching her against that coat of his.

"No!" Igraine screamed, splaying her hand toward him.

"You...can...not...have...her," Mordred said, crying out as the light lashed at him again.

And then it seemed to Igraine that time slowed, as if such a thing could happen. She saw the old woman send a torrent of white light toward the Fae Lord, and she saw him summon a great wave of green light, like a writhing mass of twisted vines. They were hurtling toward not the one who harmed him but to Igraine. She turned to face it, to see the wash of his wrath when Arthur pushed her out of the stranger's grasp. His body was struck instead, lashed and snarled with vines made of the foul light.

He turned his head toward her and whispered, "I love you." The vines pulled him to the ground where he lay still.

"Arthur," Igraine screamed, falling to her knees. Just down the road, Mordred had dropped to his knees as well, mirroring her crumpled body. Blood spilled on the road near him, and he fell to his side. The child cried, sobbing into the sleeve of the old woman.

"Hush, love, hush. He will live, Lowen. He will live."

Igraine's own tears splattered Arthur's face, his closed eyes wet as she kissed his forehead and cheeks. Hands were pulling her up, drawing her away from him.

"No, no, I won't leave him," Igraine cried.

"Hush now, it will be well. We'll tend to him and to you. We must get you home."

As the child took Igraine's hand and led her down the road, she heard the old woman say, "We made things right, Arty. You can go home."

CHAPTER THIRTY-THREE

"You have great magic, Morgan. As strong as your mother, maybe stronger. Perhaps as strong as me, in time." Nimue said as they prepared to leave the Kieve. Merlin was already astride his horse, though Morgan wondered how he had the strength to hold on. The spell had taken almost everything he had out of him.

"I felt it working. I felt the blow that struck Mordred and the power that ebbed against him. But after that, I felt something else. Did you also? A powerful magic, something I've never felt before, almost like an echo inside me. I can't explain it." They were standing in almost complete darkness, but she could see the glow of Nimue's dress against the water's edge.

"Yes, I felt it as well. In time, I think you will learn its source. For now, it is enough to know that Mordred has failed in his purpose. I do not think this is the end of danger from him, but we have earned a respite. Come, we must get you and Merlin home. He, too, will need to be healed. There has been dark magic worked by his hands, and it has damaged him more than he knows."

Nimue led her to her horse, holding the bridle as Morgan mounted the stirrup. "I journey from this place to an isle not far from here, and I would have you join me. I could teach you about your history, and about the magic, you have yet to learn. We could tend to your baby when she is born." Nimue smiled.

"What baby?" Morgan asked, looking down at the white gown as it faded back toward the water in the darkness.

"Find me at Avalon when you are ready," Nimue said, and the shadows drew her in.

♛

THEY CROSSED the landbridge leading back to Tintagel, and the clouds had finally broken, with the moon shining on the gray stone turris. Merlin had said little on the ride back, and that was just as well because Morgan was trapped in Nimue's words. *We could tend to your baby when she is born.*

"Morgan, we still must deal with Ithyl. I will need your help because I am depleted. Together, we should be able to deal a swift blow. It is dark magic, but it serves a greater good."

"No," Morgan said without hesitation. "Enough. I will see to Igraine, but I will not kill Ithyl. And you do not have the strength to hurt him, not now. You must heal, or it will be your end. Geraint must deal with his brother, now that Mordred is not his guardian."

She expected Merlin to argue, to demand that she listen to him and do what he said, but he did not. He walked his horse toward the stables and carefully climbed down. Though he looked unsteady on his feet, she was pleased to see his limp was almost gone.

"As you say, Daughter. Let's tell King Geraint."

♛

GERAINT PACED the Great Hall as they entered with his loyal men ringing the edges of the room. It had been a sleepless night for the King of Dumnonia.

"Merlin, you're back. What news?"

The pair crossed the silent hall, and the king gestured for Merlin to join him on a bench before he answered. "Ithyl's ally is defeated, for now. He has no magic to protect him. You and your soldiers can strike him without fear."

"Simon, fetch Lord Ithyl to us. We would have words now." The page scurried from the room. "Men, as your king and rightful ruler of this land, I ask you to stand against the traitor Ithyl and his followers. For those who stay loyal to the throne, there will be great rewards."

As the men murmured around us, Geraint leaned in to whisper, "And what of Igraine? Is she safe?"

"Mordred will not be able to harm her. I will go fetch her from the barrow myself," Morgan said. "The price though, is that you let Igraine decide her future. She shall say what becomes of her life, not you. Do you agree?"

Geraint nodded, and they said nothing more until Ithyl and his bodyguards came into the hall.

"It is not dawn, Brother. Have you decided already?" Ithyl looked like a man who had been roused from his bed. *How easily he was able to sleep, thinking himself secure, Morgan marveled.*

"Ithyl, your Fae Lord cannot save you. Magic will not protect you from harm today. Nor will you harm my daughter. She is free from danger as well. It seems your leverage over me is at an end. Now, do you still wish to press this claim?" The soldiers near the walls began to stomp their feet, filling the space with the rattle of swords. Ithyl's men tightened their ring around him.

"How do I know you speak true, Geraint? This could all be a ruse." Ithyl still sounded easy in his tone, but Morgan could see the worry on his face.

"Call for him. See if he comes to your aid. I will wait."

Ithyl stared at his brother, and the room grew restless. Despite his earlier words of settling this like men, without the need for magic, he'd clearly counted on Mordred to enforce his demands. Without him, Ithyl was a wise enough soldier to know that many would die, perhaps himself, in this fight. The odds were now against him.

"Geraint, I would bid we talk, away from the men. I believe we can reach an accord. I wish no harm to you or Igraine, just as I wish no harm to Laria and our unborn child. Let us speak, as brothers."

Morgan turned to see what the king would do. He could have easily demanded Ithyl thrown in chains. As king, he could have slain him right there on the floor of the hall. The old king's milky eyes stared back at his brother, brows furrowed.

"Come, we will go to my chamber, with Merlin, and I will hear your terms. Tell your men to disperse and lay down their arms. There will be no peace without that." Geraint stood up, with Merlin joining him, and the pair walked toward Ithyl's circle. As exhausted as he was, Morgan knew Merlin would be ready with a spell should Ithyl make any move.

Ithyl hesitated only a moment and then whispered something to a soldier near him. The circle disbanded, and the soldier placed his sword on the floor, with the rest of Ithyl's men following his lead.

"Morgan, wait until I come back, and we will ride to get Igraine together. I owe her that." Merlin said before following the king and his traitor brother from the hall.

♕

MORGAN HAD BARELY EATEN before the king and Merlin returned. Whatever negotiations had been made, it hadn't taken them very long. Ithyl was not with them.

"Where is he?" Morgan took a final sip of her ale.

"He is rousing Laria. They depart the castle at dawn. They are exiled from the kingdom, beyond the Veil, to live out their lives."

"That was merciful," Morgan said, having her own doubts at the king's judgment. *What would stop Ithyl from raising an army to strike against Dumnonia?* The Veil was intact for now, but it might not stay that way.

"I told him that if Igraine decides to leave, I will make his child my heir. Any treason on his part and no mercy would be shown to him or his family." Geraint stepped upon the dais and sat on his throne; he looked as worn as Merlin.

The doors to the Hall opened, and Igraine stepped in, alone, covered in dirt, her gown torn at the hem. *How in the world had she made it away from Mordred's barrow on her own, and where was Arthur?*

"Igraine, thank the goddess you are safe. We were just about to fetch you," Geraint said as she strode across the room toward them. Morgan smiled at her, but only stony coldness greeted her back.

"Arthur is dead," she said. "Mordred killed him. He took a blow that was meant for me."

Morgan gasped at her words. She never wanted any harm to come to Arthur. Morgan knew how much Igraine loved him and how deep this pain must hurt her. Her heart ached for her, and she wanted to go to her, to comfort her, but Igraine's stern gaze kept her rooted where she stood. She wanted no condolences.

"I had a long walk to think about things, and I have decided what will happen. I will return to Tintagel. There is nowhere in the world for me now beyond these walls. I will stay here and raise this child. I will raise him to be a good ruler, a king of his people. This will keep the kingdom safe behind the Veil. But I demand three things." Her face had never looked so hardened before. The Igraine that Morgan had known, the young girl who liked to sit in the garden with her cat was gone, likely forever. This was a woman of wrath before them.

"What do you ask?" Geraint spoke, but Igraine turned to look at Merlin.

"First, you must teach me, teach me everything you know, every spell I want to learn, every dark secret I want to master. Nothing shall be forbidden or unknown to me. Do you swear this?" Merlin nodded, and her own nod accepted his answer.

"Second, the prophecy says that my child must be sacrificed to save his people. This, I cannot permit. I will raise him and teach him and let him serve as king, but you must find a way to thwart any sacrifice for him. My child will be known as Arthur, and will not be harmed. Do you swear this?" Morgan looked at Merlin to see what he would do. *What guarantee could he make to keep Igraine's child from harm's way?*

"I will do everything in my power to protect him, even if it means my life," Merlin said, and she nodded at him.

"I bind you to that oath, Merlin. And third, Morgan is to be banished from the kingdom, never to return. Arthur and I trusted her word, and it caused his death. I never want to see her again. Do you swear this?" She never once looked at Morgan, keeping her eyes fixed on Merlin's face. *Would he be able to swear to never see me again to suit Igraine's demands?*

"I swear it," he said, turning to look at Morgan, tears trickling down the lines on his cheeks.

"Then, I will honor my pledge and stay at Tintagel. Morgan must be gone before I return from my chamber." Without another word, she turned and left them in the Hall.

"Morgan," Merlin said, but she held up her hand. There was nothing to say. He had made his choice, and it was Igraine and her child. She would find another path, away from this place.

"It is alright — time for me to explore the world. Perhaps I will join Nimue at Avalon, at least for a while. I am not angry, Merlin. I am sad, but I understand. Some things are bigger than one person. The babe's fate cannot be denied." Igraine had called the baby Arthur, and it seemed right to Morgan that she should honor her lost love that way. Even in Igraine's fury, Morgan didn't hate her or her choices. Maybe one day, they would make peace.

"Forgive me," Merlin said, and she nodded before turning her back on him and the king. She would take her horse and find her way to Avalon.

CHAPTER THIRTY-FOUR

1984

Lowen and Arty stepped through the portal, and a splatter of rain struck him in the face. A spring squall was in full force back at the castle ruins.

"What happens now?" Arty asked, picking his watch up from where he had left it on the stone rock. The band was soaking wet.

"You go back to your life. Like Mum told you, you are destined for great things, Arty. You'll be a leader of your people, help change the world. Go do that. That is what Mum wanted for you." The rain plastered her hair like a mat to her head, and he finally noticed that her eyes had none of the innocence of a child. Her face looked like someone who had seen far too many years.

"And what about you?" Morgan had been too weak to risk traveling back with them. She was going to find a safe space in some place she called the Kieve. She couldn't risk going back near the castle.

"I'll go back to be with Mum, at least for a while. Once I know she's safe, maybe I'll come back here. Maybe not. I don't know. Mum won't live forever, I know that. Her human blood makes her age. I have a trace of it in me, but my father's blood means I age ever so slowly. You'd never have guessed I was a thousand years old, would you?" She smiled that impish grin and turned back toward the portal.

"Lowen, will I see you again or Morgan? Is this really all over?" Arty's life was at the bottom of this hill, away from these ruins, but he couldn't believe that he was done with their story, done with Igraine and even poor Arthur.

"Oh, Arty, you never know what the future holds. It just might surprise you," she said, and she was gone.

IT HADN'T WORKED. Lowen had tried to change things, tracing things back to the point where everything originated, but everything still happened. Just as before.

Her mother had saved Igraine the first time, and Lowen made sure she couldn't do that again because her father had told her to. *But Mother found another way. She found Arty, and had him save Igraine.* Lowen had trusted that her mother knew best. But when Morgan struck down Lowen's father, on the road like a dog, she knew that wasn't true. Everything had just been revenge for Morgan, Lowen could see that now. Actions designed to hurt Mordred... *I love my mother, but I am my father's daughter.*

Going back to change the past hadn't changed Lowen's future or prevented her father's wounds. Just because she had failed once, though, didn't mean she had to fail again, she reasoned. Lowen could always go back and try something else. The next time, she would be older and more powerful. She would have more of her father's training. This next time would be different.

AUTHOR'S NOTE ON HISTORICAL REFERENCES

The Dark Lady of Tintagel is a fantasy story, but there are historical references within for fans of early Britain. The Kingdom of Dumnonia existed in post-Roman Britain from roughly the fourth century to the eighth century, in modern Cornwall and Devon. Similarly, the lands referenced as Ceredigion, Mercia, and Wessex were all historic regions during this period.

For those familiar with the Arthurian legends, you may have been struck at some of the changes in the story - the parentage of Morgan and Mordred most especially. I took inspiration from the fact that these tales evolved over time, with characters like Morgan le Fay changing to suit the author's needs. It may not be canon, but it is an homage to the evolution of these stories.

A few other notes: Hereca, the sailor on *The Gloria* with the elongated skull, is based on historical records of the Huns practicing cranial manipulation. The Hunnic Empire is fascinating, and though the empire did not exist by the time of our story, I felt sure that many of the customs would have survived. Hereca's story will be explored later in the Queens of the Mist series.

King Geraint was based on a figure who ruled Dumnonia until 710 A.D. Merlin, who is a character of my own creation, is interesting in the Arthurian legend because he too may have been inspired by a historical person. For further reading, check out the name of the ancient Welsh poet, Myrddin Wyllt.

To those familiar with the land features of Cornwall, I hope you permit poetic license with my map of Dumnonia. Things may look a little different behind the Veil.

Look for Book Two in the Queens of the Mist series coming soon.

CAST OF CHARACTERS

Court of Dumnonia at Castle Tintagel - 684 A.D.

- Geraint - King of Dumnonia, a land to the west of Anglo-Saxon Wessex, with its high seat at the Castle Tintagel
- Igraine - Princess of Dumnonia, Geraint's only child
- Ithyl "the Rock" - brother of King Geraint
- Laria - Ithyl's new wife
- Gisela - Lady-in-Waiting to Princess Igraine
- Edith - Presides over the kitchens of the Castle Tintagel, mother of the sailor named Arthur "Spear"
- Uther Pendragon - Prince of the northern kingdom of Ceredigion
- Merlin - Sorcerer to King Geraint
- Morgan - Daughter and apprentice of Merlin

Crew of *The Gloria*, a trading vessel sailing between Castle Tintagel and Constantinople

- Arthur "Spear" - son of Edith, born at Tintagel and childhood friend of Igraine.

- Hereca - crewman aboard the ship, female sailor and pirate

The Unseelie Court of the Fae:

- Mordred - A Prince of the Unseelie Court, a Dark Fae
- Queen Eithne - Ruler of the Unseelie Court
- Nimue - Seer and Dark Fae

Modern Ruins of Tintagel, Cornwall, U.K. (1984)

- Arty Drake - Archaeology student from Seattle, Washington, visiting the ruins of Tintagel
- Elsbeth - Archaeology student on the site of Tintagel
- Porsche - Archaeology student on the site of Tintagel
- Lowen - Young girl about ten years old, lives at the ruins with her mother

ABOUT THE AUTHOR K. A. MILTIMORE

K. A. Miltimore lives in the Pacific Northwest and writes paranormal cozy mysteries, modern witch lit tales, and historical fantasy fiction in the wee hours of the morning. She loves mid-century fashion, 80s music and nachos (not necessarily in that order).

With her husband and son, she loves exploring quirky local towns, including Enumclaw, WA (the setting of her Gingerbread Hag series). Perhaps she will succeed in dragging her family to Iceland for a tour someday.

She fancies herself a crafty person, both in projects and devilish schemes. In addition to a love of writing, she has a Masters in Labor & Employment Law that she is still paying off, a fondness for great Washington red wines, and re-watching the movies that she has forgotten over the years.

She is especially drawn to fiction with strong female characters, elements of magic and the supernatural, and plenty of quirky characters. Maybe that is why she tries to fill her stories with the same things that she loves as a reader.

#MagicLife is more than just a social media tag; it is a lifestyle motto. KA believes there is always magic that can be found in the mundane, if we only look, because magic is all around us.

BOOKS BY THIS AUTHOR

Burned to a Crisp - A Gingerbread Hag Mystery

Nestled deep in the sleepy heart of Enumclaw - a little town in Washington state - Hedy Leckermaul owns a bakery renowned for its strange, sugary confections. Unbeknownst to the town, she also hosts mysterious visitors. Hedy, Adelaide the ghost, and Hedy's menagerie of animals, offer a place of safety to Enumclaw's supernatural travelers. Life in the little town in the shadow of Mount Rainier may appear picturesque, but things are often not as they seem.

Peace and tranquility rarely last, and it isn't long before arson and abduction rock the friendly town, turning the bakery's world upside down. Hedy must think fast when one of her own is now in danger. She has to solve the mystery before it is too late - seconds count before you are Burned to a Crisp.

If you like mysteries with talking animals, paranormal cozy stories, fairy tales, mythology and a hefty dose of cookies, you'll love Burned to a Crisp.

In the Teeth of It - Book Two of A Gingerbread Hag Mystery

It's been two months since the fiery events of Burned to a Crisp, and it's Christmas in Enumclaw. Hedy is back to hosting visitors in her waystation, while Mel and Darro are decking the halls and telling tales of Krampus in between batches of cannibal Gingerbread Men cookies—just another Christmas at The Gingerbread Hag bakery.

But the holiday spirit isn't the only thing making its way through Enumclaw. Something definitely from the naughty list is attacking the local farms and the children are possessed with mischief. Hedy's worries increase when the Concierge sends someone to investigate her house and possibly shut the waystation down for good.

Who's been naughty, and who's been nice? Not every gift under the tree is one she'll want to open, but Hedy better hurry, before all of Enumclaw gets caught In the Teeth of It.

Sweet Tooth and Claw - Book Three of A Gingerbread Hag Mystery

Snow blankets sleepy Enumclaw just before Valentine's Day and threatens to derail all of Hedy's efforts. Demonic cupid cookies and pierced heart cakes may go uneaten, but that's hardly the worst of it. Romantic woes of her own and long-lost friends from the past bring danger that could turn this Valentine's Day blood red for everyone she loves. Revenge is a dish best served cold, but will a fiery temper hellbent on retribution send everyone at the Gingerbread Hag bakery to its breaking point? Twists, turns, and betrayal make this a winter holiday that Hedy would like to forget. A Sweet Tooth and Claw might mean the end of her little supernatural waystation and so much more.

"An exciting instalment to the Gingerbread Hag series that encapsulates the best parts of cozy mystery and fantasy into one novel. A brilliant read that I recommend to everyone!" - Jamie Kramer, Books and Ladders

Pink Moon Rising - A Witches of Enumclaw Book

DANGER AND REVENGE ARE POTENT INGREDIENTS IN A SPELL THAT JUST MIGHT END HER COVEN FOR GOOD.

Helen Griffith and her fellow witches in the Sisters of the Crescent Moon coven, are hosting the annual Eve of May Festival in nearby Ravensdale. It is a great honor for the little group. But weeks before the big event, one of their own is stricken with a mysterious illness. Could she be cursed? What witch would risk such a thing? Banishment or worse awaits anyone who would dare to curse a fellow witch.

In their search for answers, Helen and the coven seek out a banished recluse, the High Witch of the Pacific Northwest and, as a last resort, they'll even infiltrate another coven to discover the truth. The Sisters and their familiars will find trouble during the rise of the Pink Moon, when someone is determined to keep her secrets buried - whatever the cost.

From the world of the Gingerbread Hag Bakery, a new series: Pink Moon Rising - Book One of The Witches of Enumclaw. Perfect for fans of Witch Lit or Urban Fantasy, get ready because the witches are coming.

The Necromancer and the Chinchilla - Short Stories from The Gingerbread Hag Bakery

Five short stories that tell tales from the lives of characters in Burned to A Crisp - A Gingerbread Hag Mystery. Find out a little history for Maurice, Alice and Zelda, Adelaide, Darro and Hedy. A little dessert for after you have finished reading Burned to A Crisp - A Gingerbread Hag Mystery.

Stories include:

The Necromancer and the Chinchilla

Adelaide Meets a Hippie

That Time Zelda Ate Alice

Hedy in the Big Easy

Granny Raith Kills Maryjane

Creating Cinderella

Contributing Author

Twelve fresh takes on the Cinderella fairy tale with the net proceeds going to Australian wildlife relief. Creating Cinderella - Retold Fairy Tales is a collection of new and innovative stories, turning the Cinderella tale we know on its head. Explore these new stories and discover the power of transformation as each tale takes on the legend.

Printed in Great Britain
by Amazon